F. Bayford Harrison

The Ideal Artist

A Novel: Vol. I.

F. Bayford Harrison

The Ideal Artist
A Novel: Vol. I.

ISBN/EAN: 9783337064969

Printed in Europe, USA, Canada, Australia, Japan

Cover: Foto ©Andreas Hilbeck / pixelio.de

More available books at **www.hansebooks.com**

THE IDEAL ARTIST

A NOVEL

BY

F. BAYFORD HARRISON

. . . . . Love—
A more ideal artist he than all.
TENNYSON.

IN THREE VOLUMES.

VOL. I.

LONDON:
HURST AND BLACKETT, LIMITED,
13, GREAT MARLBOROUGH STREET.
1893.

THE IDEAL ARTIST.

CHAPTER I.

THE QUARREL.

I am faint
Talking of horrors that I looked upon
At last without a shudder.
The City of the Plague. JOHN WILSON.

THE nineteenth century began on 1st January, 1801. This is a fact important to remember, because many persons imagine that it began on 1st January, 1800; such persons think that 31st December, 1799, was the last day of the eighteenth

B 2

century, and they suppose that 31st December, 1899, will be the last day of the nineteenth century. And yet if you set them to count a hundred they would not stop at 99, nor begin the next hundred with 0.

So it was on one of the first nights of this current century, that a party of young men sat drinking and playing cards in a large room of a house near St. James's Street. Not only did they drink and gamble, but they also swore. Their language, if reported, must be largely interspersed with dashes; for George III. was king, and George, Prince of Wales, was at loggerheads with his father, separated from his wife, the very ideal of a spendthrift and a debauchee. And in those good old times the fine old English gentleman used oaths as strong as his port. I am not sure that the English gentlemen of the present day, when unrestrained by the presence of ladies, always speaks in the style suitable for the Sunday-school; but I am quite sure that he lives a life purer, gentler, healthier, more godly, righteous, and sober than did his immediate forefathers.

I shall first show you a little picture of an occurrence at the beginning of the nineteenth century, and afterwards spread out a wider canvas dated in the last decade of the same century; and you may compare and contrast as you will. And I think you will prefer the morals and manners of our own days to the morals and manners of the good old times.

The room in which six young ' bloods ' were assembled that dark winter night

was one at the back of a large house, which
was known as the rendezvous of half the
wild fellows of fashionable life, and as the
place in London where more money was
lost, and more duels were arranged, than
any other ten places which you could name.
The company was not so numerous as it
had been a couple of hours earlier. Two
men had been taken away in a helpless
condition and in hackney coaches. Two
others had staggered out to ' box the watch '
in Piccadilly. Several had fallen asleep
on benches. Five others were still playing
cards at a green-baize covered table.

One of these youths was tall and fair,
with regular features and hair of a hue
just escaped from red. The powder had
fallen out of this hair, and its natural
colour re-asserted itself, adding brightness

to a face which was delicate and interesting more than strictly handsome. There was a flush on the cheeks and a thickness in the voice, but the young man was not drunk. He had been playing cards recklessly for some hours, and had received I O U's many and various. His luck had been great and constant; so great that at last only one man would continue to play with him, and then the fair lad began to lose, and lost more than he had previously won.

His adversary was a few years older than himself, shorter, stouter, darker; he was also handsome; of an olive-hued skin, and brilliant dark eyes; his wig tied behind with a black ribbon concealed his hair. Rings glittered on his fingers; to a heavy chain was hung an enamelled and jewelled and coronetted watch. He was a more dashing figure than his opponent, but not so pleasing.

' Will you play any more ?' asked the dark man.

' Certainly,' replied the other ; ' —— it, I am not one to run away because the luck turns. What do you say to some —— écarté ?'

' I say yes, by ——,' returned the dark one ; ' and may your bad luck last an hour longer, Charley, my dear boy !'

' Thank you for nothing,' retorted Charley.

The other three men stood looking on while Charley and his friend played écarté ; and shouts resounded of ' I back Charley !' ' Two to one on Frank !' and of expressions too strong for record.

Almost immediately Charley began to win. And he continued to win. He held the king, or turned up the king, time after time. Frank's face grew darker, and his expressions stronger; his ruffles were torn, his whole dress disordered, his glass emptied oftener and oftener. As for Charley, though excited and noisy, he was far less so than his opponent. His luck was something wonderful; the stakes were doubled, quadrupled, still he won; the blue light of dawn begun to peep coldly in at the curtained windows.

'Shall we stop?' asked Charley.

'Twenty dashes, no,' cried Frank; 'I won't let you off till I've won everything back.'

'That you won't do. I'm in luck, and I shall keep in luck.'

' How do you do it?' asked a bystander;
' what is your secret?'

' Secret?' echoed Frank; ' yes, he must have a thirty dashes secret to win like this. Lumsden, where does he keep the king?'

Lumsden only uttered a mild couple of dashes, and said that he did not know.

' What do you mean by " keeping the king"?' Charley said, as he paused in the middle of a deal.

' I mean what I say, double-dash you.'

' If I thought you meant——'

' Think what you like,' said Frank, gulping down another glass of brandy.

' Then I think that you mean something offensive.'

' And what if I do?'

' Say that you do, and——'

'Gentlemen,' interposed Lumsden, 'no quarrelling, if you please. Remember that you are cousins.'

'Is a man to insult me because he is my cousin?' shouted Charley.

'Is a man to cheat me because he is my cousin?' roared Frank.

'*Cheat?* you say *cheat?* Forty thousand dashes! Then take that!'

And Charley threw the pack of cards full into his cousin's face.

This was a serious matter, and the by-standers saw that it was a serious matter. The insults which had passed between the cousins could only be atoned for by blood. The young men knew this. They were in a measure sobered. Both grew deadly pale. Both panted with excitement. Their teeth were set, their eyes glared. They faced each other with the table between them.

'Come, come,' said Lumsden, a heavy, good-natured little fellow, 'make it up, don't quarrel. Dash me, cousins can't fight. You *must* make it up.'

'He called me a cheat,' said Charley, doggedly.

'He threw the cards in my face,' said Frank, furiously.

'Forgive and forget,' said Lumsden.

'Excuse me,' put in another of the by-standers, 'this is not a matter which can be so easily settled. Both gentlemen have behaved in a manner which cannot be overlooked. Such a word as " cheat," and such an assault as we have witnessed, call for an explanation. Unless both gentlemen apologise, I, for one, do not see how the honour of either can be vindicated.'

'You are right, triple dash it,' said the fifth man.

'But they are cousins,' said Lumsden; 'a man can't put a bullet into his own cousin-german, Captain Butler.'

'I think he can when honour demands it. I have perhaps had more to do with affairs of honour than any one of you gentlemen. I have been out five times myself, and I have been witness in a vast number of encounters. And I say emphatically that I never saw a case in which bloodshed was more urgently demanded on both sides.'

He walked to the window and drew up the blind, showing a murky, dull, winter morning.'

'Certainly,' said Frank, 'I shall not

tamely endure such an assault as has been made upon me. Captain Butler, will you act for me in this matter?'

The captain bowed. He had to keep up his reputation as a fire-eater, and if he could not himself fight he must set other men to do so. He saw that young Frank was wrought to a high pitch of rage by wine and indignation, and he also saw that Charley was nerving himself to the deed of blood which it seemed must take place. Frank's dark face was flushed and eager; Charley's was pallid and resolute. Butler drew Frank to the further end of the room : a loathsome room it was in the wintry light, strewn with soiled cards and empty bottles; the furniture thrown here and there; the oil-lamps expiring; the air poisoned by the fumes of wines and spirits;

the men within it disordered as to raiment, haggard as to complexion, and bloodshot as to eyes. The sleepers had roused up, sick and thirsty, dirty and limp. The landlord, a mangy old fellow, had come blundering in, only half awake; a waiter had ventured inside the door, half-asleep. For the word *duel* had been uttered and repeated as if by diabolic echoes.

Lumsden took Charley by the arm, and led him towards the door.

'I say, do you want to fight your cousin?'

'Not I,' said Charley, 'if he will apologise.'

'He won't do that; Butler won't let him. Besides, you know, you were just as bad as he was.'

'He began it.'

'True.   But a word could be taken back; you can't take back a whole pack of cards.'

'He called me a cheat; let him apologise.'

Charley was sulky and sullen; Lumsden uttered several dashes, and shrugged his fat shoulders.

Captain Butler suggested no apology or compromise; the men must fight.

.' Of course,' said Frank, in a loud tone; ' perhaps he won't fight, a cheat is always a coward.'

' And at once,' pursued Butler; ' it is still early; we can call a couple of coaches and drive out beyond Knightsbridge. I know a quiet field just the other side of the village. The landlord keeps pistols always handy. I and Pratt will be your seconds; Lumsden will act for your cousin. I'll arrange with him at once.'

The captain went up to Lumsden, who agreed that certainly their men must fight.

'Neither can shoot a bit,' he added, 'they won't hurt each other. One shot on either side will be enough.'

'Probably,' answered Lumsden.

The landlord was almost in tears, deploring his hard fate, that his quiet little supper-rooms should be made the scene of a deadly quarrel, and that perhaps attention should be drawn to his house, and the police be set on him, and the affair get into the papers, and ruin ensue. To all which laments neither Lumsden nor Butler made any rejoinder. They threw the old man two or three guineas by way of payment for what had been drunk, and they went down into the street to call hackney coaches.

A coach with a couple—one could not call them a pair—of ill-fed, shambling horses, came up at Butler's call. The driver, in rough beaver hat and voluminous capes, knew by intuition the errand on which his fares were bent.

'Chalk Farm, sir?' he enquired, in a confidential tone.

'Knightsbridge!' said Butler, as he put young Frank in among the musty cushions and damp straw. Pratt followed his principal, and then Butler got in. The unwilling door was shut, and they lumbered away westward.

Another coach was summoned for the other man. Lumsden took a friend, Sinclair by name, with him, and called in Half Moon Street for a brother of his, a young doctor who was struggling to make a practice without partnership or introduction, struggling to do what is impossible. A few words from Lumsden put his brother *au fait*, and the surgeon, with a small case of instruments and lint, joined the party in the second coach.

Many a little maid-of-all-work, as she hearthstoned the doorstep of some suburban villa, gazed after the two vehicles and guessed that two gentlemen were on their way to Kensington, there to shoot each other. For such events were not of uncommon occurrence, and no one thought very much of them. In fact, duels were necessary evils like those provoking tinder-boxes, and those long bell-pulls which came down if you were in a hurry or a bad temper; all these things and many others caused a great deal of trouble, but there was no remedy, they never could be remedied; as long as the world should last, bell-pulls, tinder-boxes, and duels must continue to trouble the world. How could a man vindicate his honour, his honesty, his truthfulness, except by standing up to be shot at? For instance, how could young Charley prove that he had not cheated at cards, except by making himself a target for his cousin to fire at? If he went out this cold, foggy morning in a field at Kensington, and allowed Frank to put a bullet into him, then all his friends would know that he never had cheated at cards. The thing was perfectly plain. A man must possess every virtue

under the sun if only he could face death.
And if ever Englishmen should take any
other means to prove their probity, or to
avenge an insult, than this means of duelling, then indeed England would go to the
dogs and never return.

Thinking thus, and reflecting on the
intimate connection between virtue and
duelling, the silent party in the second
coach were jolted along to Knightsbridge
and beyond. In the other coach a conversation was sustained by Captain Butler
with little assistance from his principal or
from Mr. Pratt. The retired officer had
many tales to tell of his prowess, not on
the field of battle, but in single combat.
He had ghastly details, over which he
gloated, of men shot through the heart;
of men winged; of sword encounters in

which accidentally noses and ears were sliced off. At length, seeing Frank grow paler and paler, Mr. Pratt begged Butler to cease his dash-dashed yarns, and try to look cheerful. This the warrior was the more ready to do, as at this moment they arrived at the furthest point to which he intended that they should drive. They alighted at the entrance to a muddy lane; presently the second coach came in sight, and then the two parties, with a space between them, walked up the lane, and through a little wood.

CHAPTER II.

THE DUEL.

Then said the Squyer, courteouslie,
Brother, I thank you heartfullie;
Of you, forsooth, I nothing crave,
For I have gotten that I wold have.
                                SIR DAVID LYNDSAY.

THEY had passed a farm on their way up
the lane, and though the inmates made
a shrewd guess as to the business which
brought half-a-dozen gentlemen out into
the country on a winter's morning, they
did not offer to interfere even from curi-
osity. There were a good many meetings

at the other side of the wood; the gentlemen mostly fired in the air; and, if it
amused them to do so, why should peace-
able farmers and market-gardeners trouble
themselves about such matters?

It was a deplorable scene in that open,
muddy, spongy, grass field. The prin-
cipals took off their great-coats, and stood
in their evening suits, the one in bottle-
green with lace at his neck and wrist,
the other in snuff-brown, with a frill of
fine cambric to his shirt, and pink silk
stockings. Frank threw his hat to his
seconds, Charley pushed his hat back
on his head. They were both fine young
fellows, the one dark and distinguished
looking, the other fair and lovable; both
men of good family and of unblemished
character. Loved of somebody, doubtless,

both of them; was there mother or sister who would be heart-broken this day? Was there sweetheart or wife whose very life would follow that bullet which this moment has its billet to lodge in the upright, healthy frame of yonder youth? Dr. Lumsden looked at them with a professional eye. He shook his head.

'Jack,' he whispered to his brother, 'can't you stop it even now?'

Lumsden went up to Charley.

'Will you be satisfied if I get an apology from your cousin?'

'Yes, if he makes an ample and humble apology.'

Jack Lumsden walked down to Captain Butler, who was pacing the ground.

'My man has no ill-feeling against yours. If young Frank will apologise,

Charley will be satisfied. Butler, I don't fancy seeing one of these lads dead before my eyes.'

'Perhaps, sir, you are not accustomed to affairs of honour,' said the captain, with something of a sneer; 'my man will make no apology, I assure you; if either should do such a thing it is your principal.'

'Will you suggest an apology to young Frank?'

'I will, sir,' answered Butler, with an elaborate bow.

He went to Frank, and a few words passed between them; then he returned to Lumsden, pulling up the fur collar of his coat, and saying that it was the most dashed cold morning he had ever known.

'Any apology?' asked Lumsden, anxiously.

'No, sir.'

'Then they must fight?'

'So it seems.'

The ground was measured; the pistols were loaded; the men were put in position. Worn and haggard they were, unkempt, weary, a pitiable sight. Butler was to give the signal. Each man turned and fired. Frank staggered, and then fell headlong; Charley dropped on his knees, and remained crouched on the ground.

Lumsden and Sinclair flew to Charley.

'You are wounded?'

'I don't know; I think something struck me.'

'It is your arm.'

The left arm was hanging limp, and Lumsden saw that a bullet had passed through the fleshy part above the elbow.

' It is not much,' said he.

' And Frank?'

They looked at Frank. He lay on his face, Butler, Pratt, and Dr. Lumsden leaning over him.

' Can you rise?' asked Lumsden; ' I will go and see what is the matter.'

He ran to the other group, Charley following him slowly, supporting his wounded arm with the whole one, and leaning against Sinclair.

Very grave were the three men who knelt round Frank; his shirt-front was crimson, and blood came through it in spurts. His face was deathly pale, his eyes fixed wistfully wide open, his breath coming in sudden gasps. Dr. Lumsden had out his instruments and his lint, but he was not attempting to use either, his fingers were on his patient's wrist, and he looked at the others with an expression of utter hopelessness.

' Where ?' said Lumsden.

' Lungs,' returned the doctor.

' Can you do nothing ?'

' Nothing.'

At this word Charley gave a smothered groan full of all bitterness and self-reproach; his cousin heard it, and turned his eyes on his murderer.

' It was all fair,' he murmured, as fresh spurts of blood dyed his waistcoat; ' we fought fair. Good-bye, Charley.'

' Oh, Frank ! what have I done ? Save him, Lumsden, save him ! I'll give my life if you will save him.'

The doctor made a few movements as if trying if anything could be done; but it was impossible. Already life was ebbing with every gush of blood ; the eyes were sightless and growing glazed ; the breath was more difficult. Death was at hand. Charley knelt beside his cousin clasping the pallid hand which returned no pressure, calling aloud for forgiveness which could never be granted on this side of the grave. Honour was avenged for both ; Frank was murdered by his cousin. Charley was for ever a miserable man, the murderer of his cousin. A rain of tears, though he knew it not, poured down his cheeks ; he wrung his hands together, unconscious that he himself was wounded, but no contrition could recall that young life which had gasped itself away in the damp, still air.

'You must go,' said Pratt to Charley ;

' get back to the coach ; drive as fast as you can to the river and take a boat—or get into the City and jump into the first mail—but be off—fly—fly the country—your life may be forfeit.'

' Oh, take it ! take it !' groaned Charley ; ' I can't live with this on my conscience ! Why, man, I went to school with him ! I was next heir after him ! I love him ! Save him, kill me !'

But Sinclair and Lumsden seized on the wretched boy and dragged him away through the wood, down the lane ; bundled him into one of the coaches, and made the driver lash his horses and hurry them back to Piccadilly. There they found that London was rousing itself, and their wild looks might be noticed. They paid off their coachman, and hailed another vehicle, and were driven into the city, found that a mail-coach would start at noon for Dover, and took a place in it for Charley. Pratt had some bank-notes, and Lumsden some gold in his pockets; this they forced on Charley, who also had the coin which he had won, but now forgot in his agony of remorse. He did not know what they were doing; he seemed to be in a haze, a dream—a frightful dream. Not until he had fallen asleep in the coach and had been wakened by an aching sensation in his left arm, did he really know what had happened. He had only one companion inside the coach, an elderly woman who saw that he was ill and unhappy, and who pitied him. Arrived at Dover, he found that a packet was about to sail. He went on board, was carried across the Channel, and was never again seen by any of his friends or acquaintances.

The scene in the swampy field at Kensington was not of long duration. Very soon the pulse ceased, the jaw fell, and all was over. One of the handsomest, best-born, best-bred young men in England lay dead, shot through the lungs by his cousin, his dearest friend. Even Captain Butler rubbed his eyes as he gazed on the work of that fatal duel. He covered the face of the corpse with the great-coat which the poor lad had thrown aside, and he turned to the doctor and said,

'What shall we do now?'

'Who is he?' asked Dr. Lumsden; 'I never saw him before. What shall we do with him?'

'I know him well enough. He is an

only son. His father and mother will be frantic. Good people they are, living in the country on their property. We must take him to his rooms in Craven Street, and then I must write or go down to the old people. Not a pleasant task this before me, eh, Lumsden? Do you think we could get a shutter or a hurdle at the farm to carry him on to the coach? I have seen a good many of these affairs; I am sorry about this one.'

The farmer and his son supplied a hurdle; the farmer's wife and daughter looked out from a window at the sorrowful procession which passed their house on its way to the coach. All the details of this affair were gruesome. Poor Frank had been tall, and his corpse could with difficulty be laid inside the coach, and then only by twisting the feet round in an unseemly fashion. Butler and Lumsden got inside, and at each jolt of the vehicle the body of their deceased friend moved as if with life; the coat slipped off the face and revealed the beautiful though ghastly features. The long drive to Craven Street was almost more than Butler could endure; for, being a man who posed as a freethinker, he was full of superstitious terrors. He would not have walked through a churchyard at night; he would not pass beneath a ladder, he was afraid to sit down thirteen at table, or to spill the salt, or to cross knives. And because he did not believe in the immortality of the soul he did not dare to be alone with a dead body. Therefore as soon as they arrived in Craven Street, and Pratt had climbed down from the box, Butler said to him,

' You and Lumsden get it up into his room ; there are several things which I must see about.'

He went away, leaving the two other men to make all necessary arrangements. It was he who had urged Frank to fight ; but for him this fatal duel would never have taken place. He went to his lodgings, packed his portmanteau, and ran down to Brighton for a fortnight, too much cut up by what had happened to be able to face any of his usual companions in London.

Dr. Lumsden undertook to convey the sad news of the death of their only son to the bereaved parents in Worcestershire. It was a melancholy task, but he undertook

it cheerfully, for it might prove an introduction to a rich and noble family, who
could, if they took a fancy to him, push
him into good practice. And what he
thought possible did actually occur. Dr.
Lumsden of Bruton Street was, ten years
later, a fashionable medical man, and, having passed both the College of Surgeons
and the College of Physicians, was able to
attend any case of any kind.

How the duel and its awful result was
written of in the papers, and how it
was talked of in society; how the dead
man's parents grieved long and deeply;
how one fair young girl became a sour and
bitter woman, and lived out a short and
lonely life; how these events were all re-
corded in the summaries of the year; how
the titles and the estates which should

have been Frank's went away to another branch of the family ; how advertisements were drawn up and search was made for Charley; all these things are they not written in the *Annual Register* for 1801 ?   If they are not there written, it is hardly likely that they are written anywhere else.   And it is not necessary to write of them any further in these chronicles.

BOOK II.

CHAPTER I.

WILLOW GREEN.

Bravant le monde, et les sots, et les sages,
Sans avenir, fier de mon printemps,
Leste et joyeux, je montais six étages,
Qu'on est bien dans un grenier à vingt ans !
BERANGER.

IF the reader does not know Willow Green
he should endeavour to do so. It is a bit
of the country surrounded by London, and
very likely to be crushed to death by the
embraces of the monstrous city. Already
the willows have been cut down because
their branches obstructed light or air, or

fog or soot, or some other necessary of life. Already the field crossed by footpaths has been fenced round and laid out with gravel paths and iron seats. Soon its name will be altered to Willow Square, or perhaps to Queen Anne Square, or Burne Jones Gardens. And yet there is still a charm clinging to it. It is a piece of ground in the form of an extinguisher, the pointed end lies towards a high-road on which omnibuses ply all day and nearly all night, and close to which are two stations of suburban railways. On the south side are several old houses, brown, substantial, comfortable; having big trees in front and large gardens behind. On the north side there still stands a cottage, of two low storeys, even now possessing its little pleasure-grounds fore and aft; it has a synagogue as a neighbour, and also various small sham 'Queen Anne' houses; the west-end trends away towards labourers' and laundresses' tenements; and the east-end, which is the pointed end, is made picturesque by the graceful spire of a Roman Catholic church. In summer Willow Green is the resort of all the children of the neighbourhood, and also of more staid persons who can there enjoy comparatively pure air along with their novels and newspapers, their pipes and their peppermint drops.

'And a very pleasant lounge it is, Mr. Howland,' said Mr. Quekett to his friend; 'I do not know a pleasanter spot unless you go to Kew.'

'So it is, so it is, for them that uses it as a pleasure-ground; but if you was to be always on duty, Mr. Quekett, wet and dry, with prams and babbies and tarriers, and chaps and gals, and sometimes a fellow that drunk he can't find his way home, maybe you'd not think Willow Green altogether a earthly paradise.'

'True, true,' returned Quekett, ' oh, by no means a earthly paradise. As you say, them prams, and chaps and gals, and drunken fellows, makes the place a disgrace to the neighbourhood.'

'The place is well enough,' said Howland, loftily, ' and will be as long as I am keeper; and as for chaps, I don't think much of the chaps at your stoodios, nor of the girls what they call models, not models of good behaviour some of them.'

Quekett shook his head.

' A bad lot, some of 'em. Some of 'em

well enough. Them two gents in the attics ain't the worst sort. Coleman is that free and easy you'd think he was your own brother; and Vereker has a sort of Yankee way about him which seems homely-like.'

'Oh, your Coleman ain't much of a gentleman; and as for Vereker, when he puts on his grand airs, why, the Prince of Wales and the Shah of Persia can't hold a candle to him. I wonder you ain't afraid to speak to him.'

'Afraid? Ha! that would be a joke! Me that went through the Crimean War. Have you ever seen my medals, Mr. Howland? . Alma, Balaklava, and Sebastopol, them were my services. I could tell you tales of the trenches and the Redan would make your hair stand on end. Talk of being afraid of a artist to an old soldier like me !'

'I was only joking,' said Howland, looking across the Green towards the Willow Green Studios; 'there's Mrs. Quekett a-beckoning to you; but you need not go yet; I want to hear about the trenches and Sebastopol.'

'Another day, Mr. Howland; I believe there's something special for me to do this afternoon. Coleman and Vereker has both got pictures going into the Gallery.'

Mrs. Quekett was now beckoning frantically.

'Stay a bit longer, can't you, old man? What the deuce are you in such a hurry for?'

But Quekett's lofty martial demeanour

had disappeared, and he shambled away in obedience to his wife's gestures.

'I thought you were not coming,' she remarked; 'I thought perhaps you liked your tea cold, and your toast got dry with standing in front of the fire. And a boy sent out for to come in and do a job for the attics which would be a shilling in your pocket. But of course you need not do it.'

'It's all right, Rosa, I'm ready for my tea; and I'll do anything the attics wants done. It's all right.'

'It ain't all right with you and Howland gossiping out in the cold wind, and business going to wreck and ruin. It is all wrong, I say.'

'So it is,' assented Quekett, making his way down to the basement in which he and his wife had their quarters, 'it is all wrong.'

But the tea and toast established peace between husband and wife. They occupied a couple of rooms in the basement of the Willow Green Studios; Quekett was porter, and Mrs. Quekett was housekeeper, and their duties were manifold and various.

'Vereker said he should want you to help him with a packing-case, or something of that kind; and Coleman said you'd have to carry his " Windsor Castle " to the Gallery.'

'He was joking,' said Quekett; 'there never was such a chap for joking. He's always making you laugh.'

'There you are quite mistaken,' said the wife, ' Coleman never yet made me laugh. I should just like to see myself laughing at his clumsy jokes. Did you ever know me laugh at him?'

'Well, no, not exactly; not you, perhaps, but me. That apple blossom been to-day, Rosa? Now, she's a pretty girl, if you like, so soft and pink, and yaller hair. There ain't a prettier girl in London than her.'

'Then I can't say much for your taste, Mr. Quckett. A girl with freckles, and ever such a little nose, and great blue eyes that seem to be always looking at you. Call *her* a beauty, indeed!'

'Well, no, Rosa, of course she ain't no beauty; but then she is a well-behaved girl; not one of them flouncing models that comes in as bold as brass, and never gives you good day.'

'Good behaviour don't consist in pride, Mr. Quekett; when a girl is too proud to sit down in your kitchen and have a chat with you, and won't answer civilly if a gentleman makes her a compliment, why, I don't see exactly where the good behaviour is.'

Quekett shook his head.

'Want of early training, Rosa; that gal has no manners to speak of. When I said " well-behaved," I only meant that she is not so bad as some of 'em.'

'She's the worst of 'em,' said Mrs. Quekett, draining the last drop of tea into her husband's cup, ' because she's the slyest. And if you have eaten all your toast, I advise you to go up to the attics and see what Mr. Vereker wants. A shilling never comes amiss to a man. Lor, if I was to spend as much on bongbongs as you do on baccy, whatever would you think of me?'

Quekett did not attempt to reply to this unanswerable question. He slowly made his way up the wide draughty stone staircase to the very top of the high red-brick building. There, at a door, painted white originally, but latterly decorated with three figures in the attitudes of the three Swiss patriots who show so grandly on the outer wall of a house at Brunnen, Quekett paused; he smiled as he recognised Coleman, Vereker, and Sir Frederick Leighton in those three figures. He knocked, and a voice roared, ' Come in.'

The attic studio was a large room with a sloping roof and a skylight. One half of it was Mr. Coleman's ground, the other half Mr. Vereker's. On the one side everything spoke of the landscape painter; small sketch-books, boxes of water-colours, a model in cork of a water-mill, and above all half-a-dozen canvases on which trees and lakes were indicated, showed that Coleman devoted himself to the study of Nature. On the other side were bits of armour, coloured silk scarves, a lay figure, a sitter's platform and chair, and canvases bearing heads in various stages of incompleteness; and this side was Vereker's.

The two young men were at work: Vereker touching in here and there little bits of light and shade on a very pretty picture, three-quarter length, of a fair young girl holding a branch of apple blossom which seemed to tone well with her fair skin and golden-brown hair. The pose was simple, the face more interesting than beautiful.

Coleman was engaged in getting a canvas, some three feet by two, into its frame. Windsor Castle with an autumn sunset effect was the subject of this picture; not a novel subject, nor one treated in a novel manner; but sunset is always beautiful, and so is Windsor Castle, and Coleman was fairly satisfied with his work.

As to the young men themselves, Vereker was a fine height, and of rather pale, dark complexion, a good-looking man of seven-and-twenty, who struck strangers as being more of the gentleman than Coleman who was shorter, stouter, and more hirsute than his fellow-student. Both men were in holland-blouses, Coleman wearing a green velvet cap embroidered with gold, and Vereker having his thick dark hair, worn longer than is usual, in wild disorder.

'Give me your help here, Quekett,' cried Coleman to the porter; 'I can't fix this frame without assistance. Vereker there is too deadly in love with his " Apple Blossoms " to be able to succour a friend.'

'You did not ask me to help you,' said Vereker.

'Because I see you have no eyes for anyone but that young woman. I say, Quekett, don't you like my " Windsor " better than his " Blossoms "?'

'Well, Mr. Coleman,' replied Quekett, critically, ' if you ast my candid opinion I should say that your colouring is ahead of his. There's a kind of yellerness and mellerness about your sky, much like a orange, which Mr. Vereker ain't got in his gal's face.'

'But then,' said Vereker, smiling, 'don't you perceive that my girl is alive? Can't you fancy you see her blue eyes glancing at you, and her rosy lips just parting to smile at you? I assure you, Quekett, my department of art is much higher than his.'

'No doubt of it, sir; your gal might walk out of her frame she's that natural; whereas " Windsor Castle " looks as if it had never moved these thousand years, and didn't mean to move for a thousand years to come.'

'Quekett,' said Coleman, 'are you open to an offer? Will you accept the post of art critic to the *Advance Magazine?* Lots of work and no pay; quite a chance for some rising old journalist.'

' You're a gentleman as must always have his joke. Now, just let me take that frame in hand.'

As soon as with the porter's help Coleman had fixed his picture in its frame he brought out the expected shilling, saying,

' Toss you, Quekett; heads or tails? Heads you win, tails I lose. There, heads it is, so be off with you.'

When Quekett was gone, Coleman sat down by the fire and lighted his pipe; then, as the light was failing a little, Vereker put aside his palette, and threw himself into the arm-chair opposite that occupied by his friend. A silence fell upon them with the twilight. It was some time before either spoke.

'I suppose,' said Vereker, at length, 'there is no doubt as to my picture being hung.'

'How could there be?' replied Coleman, between the whiffs of smoke; 'do you suppose that Sangster and Co. would venture to reject *our* productions?'

'Not *yours*, of course, but *mine* perhaps. There's no knowing. Just as he is about to accept the " Apple Blossoms " he'll get a telegram. He lives on telegrams, does Sangster.'

'A telegraminivorous animal.'

'I hope some of them are unpleasant and disagree with him.'

'I hope so; barbed wires.'

'Coleman,' said the younger man, earnestly, 'this is a serious matter with me. If I fail to make my mark in this year's

Advance, I shall think my career at an end, and my coming to England a mistake.'

' Not a bit of it,' returned Coleman; ' a career is never at an end. A minister at eighty-three is young enough to break up an empire; a poet at eighty-two furnishes love-ditties for the rising generation; and a Yankee may go on to a hundred——'

' I'm no Yankee,' broke in the other; ' my people have always lived in Boston; I flatter myself that I have no Yankee accent.'

' Just a little twang now and then; very *piquant,* don't you know? But, I say, old chappie, why did you not stay in America? Over there they have no painters of world-wide reputation. You might have been the Perugino or the Bellini of your country.'

Felix Vereker closed his eyes as he slowly consumed a cigarette.

'I hardly know. Somehow we always thought of England as " home ;" my father and mother both had a fixed idea of spending their old age on this side of the Atlantic. But, as I have told you, my father died of disease contracted when out in the war, and my poor mother never seemed well after his death. I was a mere babe at my father's death, and only ten years old when my mother was taken.'

'I wonder where you got your talent?' said Coleman.

'From my mother's side. Her father was a fashionable portrait-painter in his day; not a Bellini nor a Perugino, nor even a Reynolds; but a respectable artist enough.'

' Did he make any money ?'

' Enough to boil the pot,' answered Vereker; ' not enough to roast the joint, had there been one to roast. And so when Lucilla Whitaker married Henry George Vereker, the son and successor of Charles Vereker, the great jute and tallow merchant, it was thought that she had made a very fine marriage. But my father was no man of business, his heart was set on military matters. The jute and tallow flared up and burnt out, and at my father's death the business collapsed, leaving a small income for my mother, which dwindled down to a pittance for me. I have left about five thousand dollars in the firm which took over the embers of the Vereker business, and, if I am ever a rich man, I shall have made my riches by my brush.'

' Five thousand—oh, not pounds, dollars—well, yours is a *dollarous* tale, my dear Felix; but you are a sly fox, and your value will be known at last by your brush. And now, as it is 6.30, what about a wash and brush-up, and dinner?'

The friends usually dined at a quiet eating-house which had a bow-window, looking out on the river; a quaint bow-window, a survival from the real Queen Anne days.

It was within Mrs. Quekett's power to cook a meal for her gentlemen, but as she had no *répertoire* beyond a beef-steak or a mutton-chop, her bill of fare was apt to become monotonous. And then, what lovely skies were seen from this bow-window! What effects of golden-brown tints! What murky splendour on the flowing Thames, what depths of mysterious shadow!

Other artists knew of this old-world restaurant, and one or two literary men, who lived out Barnes and Putney way, also took occasional meals there. And on this particular evening there was an author already seated, staring at the cruets. He was not young, nor beautiful, nor even interesting; and he was consumed by a burning desire to publish a three-volume novel, but the publishers did not reciprocate the good intentions with which he forwarded his manuscripts to them. He told many stories against himself, and seemed quite proud of his rejected attempts.

' Yes, a short tale returned from Messrs. Gryphon and Wyvern,' he said, when Coleman and Vereker glanced at the papers which lay beside him; 'and also the first three chapters of a novel which I have offered to seven publishers, who all think it extremely good and well worth publishing.'

'And when is it coming out?' asked Coleman, maliciously.

'Oh,' said the author, with much cheerfulness, 'as soon as I find a man willing to undertake it. I sometimes think it is hard that fame and fortune would be attainable if only I had a couple of hundred pounds to spare. Experts assure me that, if I were to bring out my books, I should have a great success; but they all want me to sign agreements covenanting to pay down more money than I possess. So what can I do? I will not borrow, I must save.'

He turned his attention to the sweet-bread before him.

' People think,' he continued, presently, ' that literature is such an inexpensive profession. A ream of sermon-paper, a dozen j's, a penny bottle of ink, and there you are. Scott, Thackeray, George Eliot wanted nothing more. But, when the book is written, how is it to be brought before the world? Now, you painters find things much easier. True, canvas costs more than paper, brushes more than pens, and colours more than ink. But the dealers and the exhibitions don't charge you two hundred pounds for showing your work to the public.'

' No,' said Vereker; ' but, Tothill, you do get a lot of stuff published, don't you ?'

'Oh, just a slight thing, now and then,' the author answered, very modestly; 'I got out of the *Annual Register* a list of remarkable duels, and I filled in details from Burke's *Peerage* and *Landed Gentry,* and the *Cheapside* gave me ten guineas for that. At the present moment I have an article in type for *Knock-me-down,* a paper on the *Use and Abuse of the letter H.* I am afraid it is a little over the heads of their readers, but I have counted the lines and I think it will bring me three guineas. And so we jog along! A glass of sherry,' he added, turning to the little maid in attendance, for the recital of his success had put him in a festive humour.

'Ah, Mr. Tothill,' said Coleman, with a sigh, 'literature, after all, is better paid than art. Are you connected in any way with any Daily or Weekly?'

'I have done—reports—paragraphs—for the *Monday Moon.*'

'Shall you be at the private view of the *Advance Gallery* on the 15th of April?' asked Coleman.

'I will, if I can get an order,' replied Tothill, his sallow, flabby face lighting up; 'I could do fifty lines for the *Monday Moon.*'

'I'll try to get an order for you,' said Coleman, ' and, in return, you must crack up my landscape and Vereker's figure as the finest things in the gallery.'

'Of course,' cried Tothill, 'if a critic might not pick out his friend's work for commendation, where would be liberty of judgment, or the freedom of the press ?'

And, with this poser from the author, dinner was ended, and the diners went out into the clear, cold, spring night.

CHAPTER II.

VARNISH.

—As there are heights
Seen only in the sunset, so our lives,
If that they lack not loftiness, may wear
A glow of glory on their furrowed fronts
Until they faint and fade into the night.

ALFRED AUSTIN.

THE last sitting; the last touch. The little maiden, white and pink, whose skin was as apple blossoms, sat for the last time in Felix Vereker's studio; and Harry Coleman stood once more gazing upon ' Windsor Castle,' and wondering if another gleam of yellow on the water, or another rook

against the yellow sky, would add effect
to his picture. Several times that afternoon Coleman's eyes wandered from his
own canvas to that of his friend, and he
half wished that his genius lay in the portrait line rather than in the landscape
direction. For many reasons he wished
it; one cannot sit out sketching in bad
weather; and the weather is almost always
bad for the sketcher; the sunshine is so
bright that you cannot see your subject; the
heat is so intense that your colours dry
before you can get them on your paper;
or the wind upsets your easel and
umbrella; or the dust makes everything
gritty; or the rain washes all that you
have done into a fog; or the cold numbs
your fingers so that you cannot hold
pencil or brush. But the portrait painter

does not sit out of doors; summer and winter, rain or shine, his sitters are there before him, and himself comfortably under cover. Ah! his sitters!—sometimes such sitters! The great statesman, the great scientist, the great soldier, to know such men is a privilege, and is the privilege of the great portrait painter. The noble matron, the lovely child, the beautiful girl, to gaze at such women is a rapture, and this rapture is for the portrait painter. Felix Vereker had the privilege, the rapture of gazing on Edith Crane, but he was cold, unsympathetic, unworthy of the privilege and the rapture. Vereker could calmly draw the bow of that rosebud mouth, the curve of those perfect eyebrows, could mix his yellows and greens and greys for that exquisite complexion, and yet regard the girl as only a model! While Coleman, at the other end of the room, could not turn his eyes towards Edith Crane without a palpitation of the heart, a trembling of the hand.

Now that the last sitting had arrived, and that Edith Crane was about to take her leave of Willow Green Studios, Harry Coleman began to know his own heart. He hated and despised 'Windsor Castle;' one living woman, a painter's model, the daughter of a superannuated postman, whose wife was a humble needlewoman, was worth all the royal residences in Europe. Modest, gentle, industrious, dutiful, intelligent, this lovely Edith Crane was a paragon; Harry Coleman, the seventh son of a small grocer at Whitby, determined to make a place for himself among English painters, resolved to win fame and wealth by hard work if not by sheer talent, felt himself a fitting suitor for this beautiful girl, if only he could sell his pictures and make enough money not only to boil the pot but fill it with meat and vegetables.

The last gleam of light, and the last rook being finally settled, Coleman strolled across to Vereker's easel, and watched that cold-blooded monster touching in soft shadows here and there, with no more feeling than if Miss Crane had been a martello tower, and the artist a house-agent's draughtsman.

'Your last sitting, Miss Edith?' said Coleman.

'Yes, Mr. Coleman,' replied the girl, in a pretty voice, and with little of the hard

London accent; ' all the gentlemen down-
stairs have done with me, and Nellie and
I will not have to come here any more.'

' I've got some chocolate for Nellie,' said
Vereker; ' I think I shall paint her next.
I have an idea of a Prince Arthur, and a
girl does best for a boy's head. There,
Miss Crane, I have finished; wish me good-
luck.'

He laid down his brushes.

' I do wish you good luck, sir,' said the
girl; ' I hope they will like your picture,
and buy it, and give a good price for it.'

She was putting on a cloth jacket trimmed
with shabby grey fur, and a large hat on
which some uncurled feathers stood in wild
attitudes. However much Vereker liked
her for a model, he felt the lack in her of
that inborn refinement which only comes

of heredity. Coleman, on the other hand, a true Bohemian, found the girl all that he could wish. Your true Bohemian does not nicely weigh small social differences, or even great ones; your sham Bohemian does. Coleman thought the daughter of a postman and a dressmaker quite his social equal. Nor did he feel himself inferior to Vereker, for all Master Felix's aristocratic ways. These two men had drifted together in London, and the friendship between them was that of the Bohemian brotherhood. Vereker did not perceive Coleman's intense admiration for Edith Crane.

' Good-bye, then,' said Felix to the girl, shaking hands with her; ' I do hope your portrait will be appreciated by the *Advance* people. Here is the chocolate for Nellie. Good-bye.'

He put a packet of chocolate and a packet of money into Edith's hand, and held open the door for her to pass out. Coleman had got out on the small lobby, and went down the stairs before her.

'I wish I was a portrait painter, Miss Edith. But this is not an eternal farewell. When the warm weather comes we will go out in boats, and gather water-lilies, and have pic-nics on the banks.'

Edith smiled.

'May Nellie come too? She has never been on the river? And if mother gets better she might come too.'

'I don't know if I should be equal to the whole family,' replied Coleman, rather ungraciously; 'well, good-bye, good-bye.'

These words he said in a fervent tone,

and held her two little hands, chocolate, money, and all.

Quekett was at the open hall-door, having just taken in a parcel for one of the ground-floor tenants. He beheld the adieux of these young people, and thought it a good thing that his wife did not see them ; she might have formed strong opinions and expressed them.

' Not a bad thing them sittings is over, Mr. Coleman,' said the porter, looking after Edith Crane as she walked quickly away ; ' young girls sitting to be stared at by young gents is not quite what I would like for my own daughters if I had any.'

' Why, you old Philistine, it is the best kind of life possible for a young girl.   She gets a healthy walk coming here, she gets a good rest sitting here, she gets a handful of silver for her services, and she gets another healthy walk going home. Is not that all very good for a young girl?'

' Well, yes, as you put it, Mr. Coleman; yes, I don't know as a young gal could do better.'

Mrs. Quckett's voice was heard calling to her husband not to waste his time gossiping; he took up the parcel and carried it to its owner while Coleman slowly mounted the many stairs feeling that the light was duller, and life gloomier now that Edith Crane would be no more in the joint studio.

He painted nothing that day. He hired a bicycle and went for a long ride into the country. Vereker also kept holiday. He turned over all his personal possessions; a few charms and rings which had belonged to his parents, a miniature and an old watch come down from some ancestor, a few coins and bits of china picked up on his travels, and innumerable sketches in pencil, chalk, water-colours, oils, which he knew to be of no value, and yet could not bring himself to destroy. At this time Felix Vereker believed himself destined to become a power in art, a leader in intellect; he intended to make his name in England, and then to return to America with his honours blazoned on his forehead, and a tag of initial letters after his name. Every young man who is worth his salt cherishes similar dreams, though at times his heart sinks and he moans to himself that he is a very common-place person, with only a small amount of talent, and no claim nor hope to be anything great or

even remarkable. And then he turns to
again, and picks up his brush or his pen,
his scalpel or his wig, his sword or his
trowel, and he strives on manfully towards
the unattainable heights. ' A man's reach
should exceed his grasp.' And who
would be content to think himself a
' perfect painter'?

On the day when they chartered a cab
and took their pictures to the Advance
Gallery, both Vereker and Coleman fell
into a fit of depression. The entrance of
the gallery was blocked up with pictures,
all of them the work of young men. No
man over thirty years of age could be
admitted a member of this gallery; though,
once admitted, he might remain a member
to the end of his life. The president was
Eugene Sangster, who wore his hair quite

long on his shoulders, and usually had two 'buttonholes,' a flower displayed on either side of his coat.

Eugene Sangster, P.A.G., was superintending the entrance of pictures, when Coleman and Vereker arrived with their contributions to the general mass. He was small and slight, dressed in the very neatest and nattiest suit of steel-grey, and two white narcissi shone on either side of his white satin necktie. The inventory of Sangster's peculiarities and affectations would take too much space; suffice it to say that they were numerous. He was adored and reviled, fawned upon and scoffed at; he was a bachelor, his mother was Lady Maria Sangster, he had a private income, he had talent amounting to genius, he was extremely vain, and extremely good-natured.

'There is the Pag!' whispered Coleman to Vereker; 'I have something to say to him.'

The P.A.G. was within the turnstiles, Coleman outside them. Approaching those sacred gates, Coleman said, 'How goes it, Eugene Sangster, with you to-day? Is there any hope that space may be found for my humble production?'

'Oh, yes, yes,' responded Sangster, who lisped; 'oh, yes, there may be space; I will make a note, Harry Coleman, that your picture shall be hung, if possible.' With a gold pencil set with turquoise he wrote on a sheet of pink paper. 'But, you see, we are overwhelmed with applications for space. Art is advancing; we advance it; it grows beneath our fostering influence.'

'You say sooth,' remarked Coleman; 'and do we not advance also the interests of these porters and carpenters, who so busily are employed in carrying our works of art? By my halidom, Master Eugene Sangster, you are vastly to be——'

But Harry's oration was cut short by the corner of somebody's picture being poked in between his shoulder blades. Sangster never quite knew how to receive Coleman's remarks, whether as affectation of a different kind from his own, or as impertinent jesting. Therefore the P.A.G. was not sorry to turn away and interview another aspirant to a place on the walls of the gallery.

A few days later Coleman and Vereker each received a printed notice that his picture was accepted, and that he had better attend at the gallery on the 5th or 6th of April, in order to varnish his painting and to make sure that it had not been injured in the process of hanging. On this occasion the friends took a hansom and drove up in style to the Advance. Coleman had fastened three huge bunches of primroses to the front of his coat; but Vereker had pulled them off, and presented them to Mrs. Quekett. Still, without any decorations, both young men were in high spirits, being quite confident of selling their pictures and of receiving commissions. About a hundred other artists were full of the same confidence.

No one was ' skied ' at the Advance; you were either well hung, or not hung at all. Vereker found ' Apple Blossoms ' on the line, looking very pretty and fresh and spring-like, a very taking little composition. 'Windsor Castle' was above the line, but in a capital light, and Coleman had no cause of complaint. All around were young painters with varnish, which was to improve perfection; for every picture was perfect—in theory. Eugene Sangster, wearing two great spikes of hyacinth, went about smiling and distributing cards of admission to the private view on the 15th instant.

'It is a mercy,' said Coleman to Vereker, 'that the Pag is not as great an idiot as he looks. Have you seen his "Queen Eleanor"? It is perfectly fiendish, everything wrong; but there's such stuff in it, such vigour and grandeur, that you feel as frightened as ever Rosamond did.'

'We must get our cards,' said Vereker; 'here, Sangster, I want one of your pasteboards. Oh, by George! green type on green paper. Rather a new departure, is it not? Thanks. When is the *Advance Magazine* to be started?'

'As soon as we have the sinews of war,' answered Sangster; 'we think of forming a syndicate to bring it out. It must be financed, edited, written, and illustrated by members of this gallery.'

'If you have not fixed on the editor, may I mention——'

'I shall be editor myself,' lisped Sangster.

'Then as a contributor, may I mention——'

'Everything will be judged on its own merits.'

' May I have a card for him ?'

Sangster, whose thoughts were fixed on a very large woman who had sent in a very small drawing of a tuft of forget-me-nots, gave Vereker a second card, and tripped across the room. This second card was for poor Tothill, who would ' do ' the Advance Gallery Exhibition for the *Monday Moon*, and thereby earn a few shillings.

Coleman had received his card of admission to the private view, and was standing with some other irreverent persons who found something to laugh at, not only in their small president and his large female friend of whom he evidently was much in awe, but also in each other's pictures. Smith's flesh-tints were leathery; Brown's anatomy was nowhere;

Jones's sea was pea-soup; Robinson's mountains were hard; Coleman's trees were 'green lumps lolling about the country;' Vereker's 'Apple Blossom' was grown in the Burlington Arcade; and yet, collectively, the members of the Advance Gallery formed the finest body of artists who had ever been banded together, who made the old fossils at Burlington House turn green with envy and shake in their shoes.

Greatly as the pictures differed in quality and size, in faults and in beauties, yet they differed even more in price. The P.A.G. had put two hundred pounds on his huge 'Queen Eleanor,' one hundred on his 'Toadstools,' fifty on his 'Inhabitants of the Disused Belfry.' The stout lady priced her 'Forget-me-nots' (six inches by

four) at seventy-five pounds. Coleman
hoped to get thirty pounds for his 'Windsor
Castle;' and Vereker only asked twenty
for 'Apple Blossoms.' But then, as was
often reproachfully cast at him, Vereker
was a fellow with private income.

'I don't care about a long price at first,'
he explained to Coleman, as they walked
home after the varnishing, 'I want to
make my name very quietly and humbly,
and then, when it is made, I can raise my
prices to anything I like.'

'But I,' said Coleman, 'I want high
prices first and last. I can't afford to
wait.' He was thinking of Edith Crane.

CHAPTER III.

THE DE VERES.

Why were they proud ? again we ask aloud,
Why in the name of glory were they proud ?
Isabella ; or the Pot of Basil. KEATS.

IT was commonly said of the Countess of Lillebonne that she was the proudest woman in England. She had been Lady Clara Willoughby, and proud enough as a girl ; when she married Eustace de Vere, Earl of Lillebonne, she increased in pride until she attained to such a height of haughtiness that she looked down upon every royal family in Europe. The de Veres had come over with the Conqueror, but their lineage went back in Norman records, and beyond Norman records, to times far earlier than the Christian era. The name itself was as old as Truth; *vero* is the Italian for true. The de Veres were the people of Truth, the true people. As long as Truth had existed, so long had the de Veres existed; if there ever was a time when Truth was not honoured, then there may have been a time when the de Veres were not held in honour. Why, the word *revere* pointed to the honour in which the de Veres have ever been held. Perhaps had Lady Lillebonne been born a Vere de Vere she might not so have insisted on her position.

For Lord Lillebonne was by no means

so proud as his wife; or, if he was, he was too proud to show his pride. He was an elderly man of noble presence, but afflicted with much nervousness which sometimes made him shy and awkward, and at other times drove him into a re-action of self-assertion which astonished his most intimate friends. Lord Lille-bonne was a great trial to his wife, as husbands always are to their wives. But she had to put up with him, because without him she could not have been a de Vere, or Countess of Lillebonne.

The lady had four other trials: her two sons and her two daughters. Of her sons not much need be said. The elder, Francis Edward, Lord Senlac, was quite wanting in pride, and his mother was in mortal terror lest he should marry some one out of a shop or a music-hall. He was in the Guards, and his family saw little of him. The second son, Eustace, was also in the army, but in a line regiment now quartered in Ireland; a good-natured, rather stupid and extravagant young man.

Lady Clara Vere de Vere deserves a paragraph to herself. She was tall, stately, dark-haired, dark-eyed, with a fine figure, beautiful hands and feet, and manners as haughty as her mother's. At this time Lady Clara—the eldest of the family— had passed her thirtieth birthday. No woman supposes that she looks her age; and Lady Clara believed that the world thought her younger than her brothers. Some three years previously a very unpleasant incident had disturbed Lady Clara's life. She had spent the winter

at the chief family seat, Mont Veraye,
near Malvern, and had found time hang
so heavy on her hands that she had be-
guiled it by beguiling a young farmerly
fellow of the neighbourhood into loving
her. Her beautiful dark eyes, her gentle
voice, had due effect upon the youth, and
in the hunting-field, at the County Ball,
at the parochial entertainments, he was
ever at her side. Lady Clara amused herself with his attentions, thinking no more
of them than she did of the fawnings of
her dog. But it is possible to break a
dog's heart, and it was possible to break
young Laurence's heart. One evening,
when Mont Veraye was open to an *omnium
gatherum* of Lord Lillebonne's tenants, acquaintances, and political sympathisers,
Laurence declared his love. Lady Clara

turned upon him with the one word,
'YOU!' and walked away. Laurence got
home that night. He lived in an old-
fashioned, big farmhouse with his mother,
who never went to parties. Next morning when he did not appear at breakfast
his mother went to his room. She found
him, in his evening dress, with a gaping
wound across his throat, and a photograph
of Lady Clara Vere de Vere in his dead
hand. The mother burst into wild abuse
of the woman who had murdered the beloved only son; *jilt* was the mildest term
which the miserable, bereaved creature
could bring herself to utter. It was a
wretched time for Lady Clara; there was
an inquest; the local papers used harsh
language; the neighbours gave the boy
quite a public funeral: even in London

Lady Clara's conduct was condemned; the *Monday Moon* advised her to fill up her spare time in teaching orphans to read and to sew; and the most eligible men of the next London season seemed repelled rather than attracted by her hard, dark beauty.

Lady Flora Vere de Vere was the youngest of the family, and was now just two-and-twenty. She was fair, with a delicate complexion and hair of a rich ruddy gold. Her eyes were either grey or green, or some other soft shade, no matter which. She was not a girl to discuss piecemeal; she was one to love. Having been kept back in the nursery while her sister was shown off in society, she had retained an innocence of mind and manner which drove her mother distracted, and also—though in another sense—drove several gentlemen distracted. She did not know that she had refused two or three offers; for she did not look out for such things, and her unconscious reception of the strongest hints made the hinters feel themselves rejected before they had finished urging their suits.

Lord Lillebonne posed as a patron of Art. He and his family were invited to all private views. A large pale-green card printed in large dark-green type came to him by post; with it was another of pale-blue with dark-blue type for Lady Lillebonne, and a third of pale-pink with deep rose type for the Ladies Clara and Flora Vere de Vere.

'Ha! the Advance Gallery Exhibition,' said Lord Lillebonne to the ladies; 'that is one of the most delightful functions of the spring.'

' I suppose we must go,' said the countess; ' our absence would be commented on.'

'And you will explain the pictures to me, will you not ?' said Lady Flora to her father; ' I should so like to know the difference between a good picture and a bad one.'

' The worst of these places,' remarked Lady Clara, ' is that one meets such extraordinary people. One wonders where they can have come from, and whether they are really human beings.'

' They come from studios and schools of art,' explained Lady Lillebonne, ' and it can do us no possible harm to meet them.'

So, when the day came, the party from

Eaton Place got into their carriage and drove to the Advance Gallery. There was not a line of carriages, but, ever and anon, a landau, a brougham, a victoria, drove up and deposited its occupants at the door. A stream of unfortunate people on foot was flowing continuously through the turnstiles ; and when Lady Lillebonne led her party into the first long narrow room, down the middle of which ran a sort of crystal horse-trough in which gold-fish disported themselves, she was actually pressed upon by the crowd. She put up her double eyeglass and stared at the people.

'Very strange that Mr. Sangster does not come to receive us!' she said to her eldest daughter.

And then she saw the P.A.G. struggling through the multitude. He was clothed in brown velvet—not velveteen—and his waistcoat was embroidered with gold. His flowers to-day were two full-blown Maréchal Niel roses. Sangster was anxious to revive the mediæval *décolleté* style of dress for men; and on this occasion he had gone as near it as modern prejudices and tailors would allow. He had a courteous word for the Lillebonne party; but not many such words; dukes and marquises awaited him in other parts of the gallery, and he was the host, the cynosure of London, that day, as he felt very deeply.

'I wonder who is here?' said Lady Lillebonne, when Sangster had passed on; 'I see Lady Sackbutt on the other side of the fish-pond; and I should not be surprised if we met Sir Ronald Stanley. I hear that he has returned from the East, but so changed that his own brother did not know him. Ah, Mr. Pigot, how do you do?'

Sir Ronald Stanley was supposed to be the great match of the season. His baronetcy was one of the most ancient in existence, and his income one of the largest in England; for he had been only a few months old when his father died, and the twenty years' minority had had the effect of enormously increasing his property. Lady Clara did not deign to look about for Sir Ronald, but she noted every young man whose face was unfamiliar to her. When she saw a tall, well-made fellow with an easy swing of movement, and a glance which seemed to pass over the heads of those around him, she made up her mind that he was Sir Ronald, whom

she remembered as a thick-set lad of eigh-
teen, and who must have been wonderfully
improved by his many years of sojourning
in the East. But the tall young man was
only Felix Vereker.

Lady Lillebonne's glasses fixed themselves upon a person who shocked all her
ideas of right and wrong; a person male
as to sex, shabby as to dress, eccentric as
to manner, and evidently altogether out of
his sphere. He carried a catalogue, and
made notes in it of all the pictures; some
of them he examined carefully, and of
these he wrote a good deal; others he
only glanced at, and of these he wrote
little. Lady Lillebonne at first thought
that he might be a dealer; afterwards
she came to the conclusion that he was
one of those country gentlemen who

come to town in the spring and buy up pictures at small prices, and keep them buried in the country; then when this half-crazy person dies it is found that his house contains priceless treasures of art, and his next-of-kin—he never marries—sells them and becomes a very rich man. But the shabby person was only Tothill making notes for an article in the *Monday Moon*. The countess would have been furious if she had known that Tothill had made a note of herself, her style and title, her bonnet, mantle, and gown, all for the *Monday Moon*. He was sent to notice people, as well as pictures, present at this private view.

At length Lady Lillebonne and her elder daughter subsided into seats in the upper gallery, where the great pictures of the year were arranged in artistic fantasies. A sunny landscape by the P.A.G. was placed between a large cage of canaries and a small fountain of rose-water. A moonlight view of Venice by a rising F.A.G. could only be approached through a dark closet, and only seen by the glimmer which fell through an aperture filled in with grey glass. The huge 'Queen Eleanor' was placed behind a bower twined with real ivy, and stuck about with hyacinths, jonquils, marguerites, and other flowers, all real, for the A.G. abominated anything artificial except its own President and Fellows. The 'Forget-me-nots' of the stout lady were surrounded by mirrors. In fact, as Lady Lillebonne observed to Lady Lollington, who was sitting beside her, the entire thing was got up in the manner of the Wiertz Gallery in Brussels ; quaint surprises and strange devices were sprung upon the visitor in every direction. Lady Lollington quite agreed with her friend.

' But the Musée Wiertz is a larger room than this, I think ; and I fancy they have no private views there.   I don't remember meeting anyone there whom one would care to speak to.'

' Oh, I did not mean any similarity in that way.   And I am sure M. Wiertz is not at all so charming as Mr. Sangster. Dear Mr. Sangster gets together so many nice people, and always has such very good tea.   I should think the tea-room must be open by this time.   Clara, if we could see your father and Flora we might go and have tea.'

'Yes, we might,' replied Clara, languidly; then, as ₁Felix Vereker passed just before them, she said to Lady Lollington, 'do you know if that tall, dark man is Sir Ronald Stanley?'

'Oh, dear no!' laughed the other lady, 'Sir Ronald is a little squat, dumpy fellow, who looks like a comic actor. I have no idea who that man may be. I have never met him anywhere.'

By the above scraps of their conversation it will have been seen how much these three ladies were enjoying the pictures in the Advance Gallery.

CHAPTER IV.

THE PRIVATE VIEW.

Faut-il se condamnee à l'ignorance pour conserver l'espoir ?
EMILE SOUVESTRE.

WHILE Lady Lillebonne and her daughter
Clara were enjoying the pictures after
their fashion, the Earl and Lady Flora
were amusing themselves in quite another
way. With a catalogue in his hand, Lord
Lillebonne moved slowly from canvas to
canvas, making his remarks in a low voice
to his daughter, fearful lest his praise or
his blame might wound the feelings of

some young artist. He passed by the
'Queen Eleanor' embowered in real ivy
and jonquils; he hardly glanced at the
'Venice' in the dark closet, or at the
'Forget-me-nots' among the mirrors; but
he paused before a seascape and pointed
out the movement of the water, and the
deep transparent green under the curled-
over crest of the wave.

'How do you get that transparent,
watery look?' asked Flora, in a whisper,
dreading lest anyone should overhear her
ignorance.

Of course Lord Lillebonne did not
know how to paint; he only knew how
to admire good painting.

He lingered at a view on the Thames
Embankment, in which the sun shone
more brightly than he often shines in

London. Flora wanted to know how they got that look of heat on the buildings. Again Lord Lillebonne confessed his ignorance; he supposed by contrast, or by using yellow paint. They came opposite Coleman's 'Windsor Castle;' the subject is always charming, and they stood admiring it.

Beside them came Tothill the shabby. He knew the earl by sight, and now cast about for an opportunity of speaking to him. The great disadvantage of non-success is that a man's whole heart grows to fix itself on success. And Tothill was ready to stoop to almost any vileness short of crime which might help him on his way.

'I like that very much,' said Lady Flora, as she looked up to the 'Windsor

Castle;' 'it makes one think of the summer evenings when Senlac used to take us on the river from Eton. Who is the painter?'

Lord Lillebonne had turned over two pages of the catalogue, and could not find the number he wanted. He fumbled with the leaves and grew nervous.

'I really can't tell you, I can't see; something wrong somewhere.'

Tothill saw his chance.

'Allow me, my lord; that picture is by Harry Coleman, whom I am happy to count among my friends.'

'Thank you, sir,' said Lord Lillebonne, much flurried at being addressed by a stranger.

He would have moved on, but Tothill spoke again.

' A fine work of art, and one which your lordship does well to admire. I am making notes of the best pictures, with a view to publishing them in one of the leading journals, and if I might add your lordship's opinions to my own I should be much pleased.'

' Oh, yes, no,' Lillebonne stammered, ' I really know nothing of art practically. Excuse me, I am very ignorant.'

Lady Flora, supposing Tothill to be some experienced critic, some great authority, or distinguished *littérateur*, began to listen to him with attention; which her father perceiving, lingered a little in order to please the girl. Then Tothill set to work to confuse her utterly with the shibboleths of modern art, and when he had talked for some ten minutes she was fully convinced that Coleman was the most rising artist of the day, and Tothill the most eminent of the new order of journalists.

' And if your ladyship will permit me,' he continued, ' I will point out to you one or two other pictures as magnificent in conception and as perfect in execution as Coleman's " Windsor Castle." Oh, we need not despair of art while we have such men among us. There are those who tell us that luxury is sapping the foundations of our Empire, that art can only flourish in dry and barren ground, that the increase of knowledge is the destruction of æsthetics, that it is only the ignorant who hope in the future—believe it not!'

' Thank you, sir, good-day,' said Lord Lillebonne, with one of his sudden bursts of self-assertion, as putting his hand on his daughter's arm he drew her away from the critic; 'that man is insufferable. How dare he accost you ?'

'Oh, father,' said Flora, 'I am afraid he is very poor: he has no cuffs.'

'Poverty is no excuse for impertinence,' said the earl.

'He did not mean to be impertinent, I am sure. I do wish I knew some people who really understood art !'

Tothill stood where they had left him.

'My lord,' he muttered, with his teeth closed, ' rank is no excuse for impertinence. You may look down on the poor author, but he has no such ghastly secret as you have. Everyone knows that you have in your family cupboard a monstrous skeleton, which terrifies you more than anyone else.

Now, you may lock that cupboard, and
ignore that skeleton, but if you make an
enemy of the literary man you will have
to deal with a difficult adversary. Why
should I not hunt out your secret, and
publish it? It would make splendid copy
for the "society" papers. " The Skeleton of
Mont Veraye," or of " Strathtartan Castle,"
will be a capital title.'

Tothill was quite absorbed in his rage
and his prospects of ' copy,' and stood in
the midst of the well-dressed throng, unconscious that anyone was near him. He
was recalled from his visions by the sound
of Vereker's voice.

' What is the matter?' You look as if
you were composing an ode.'

' Boys,' he said, solemnly to Vereker and
Coleman, ' there is a man here, a monster,

who requites with ingratitude my efforts to instruct his ignorant daughter.'

' Who is it ?' asked Vereker; ' but don't speak so loud.'

' He calls himself the Earl of Lillebonne,' returned Tothill; ' but I call him a conceited ass. Does a man understand art merely because he is an earl? Should a man be impertinent to literature merely because he is a peer?'

' Which is the man?' enquired Coleman.

Tothill pointed out Lillebonne in the throng; Vereker saw that a young lady was with the impertinent peer.

' He would have bought your "Windsor" presently, had he waited a few minutes longer. I had almost sold it for you. Now he has lost his chance of it, and he has made me his enemy. He does not know who I am, and how I can devour him, though he is an earl.'

'In fact,' said Coleman, laughing, 'you are the voracious vulture who will devour the early worm.'

Tothill looked superior to a pun, and walked away.

Lord Lillebonne and Flora had gone on as far as the 'Apple Blossoms.' There they made a pause, for it caught the earl's eye, and pleased him. It was, without question, a very pretty, graceful picture, and the colouring was so much that of his favourite daughter that Lord Lillebonne felt instantly much taken with it. He looked from the ruddy-gold hair in the picture to the ruddy-gold hair beneath the little green bonnet; he looked from Edith Crane's soft hazel eyes to the soft hazel eyes beside him; he saw the warm white skin on the canvas and the warm white skin of the living girl; and then it came into his mind that Flora would make a very pretty picture. Clara had been painted twice, and photographed and engraved many times; but since Flora had been grown up her likeness had not been done in any way worth preserving.

'I do like that very much,' said the father, comparing the two bright young heads.

'What a pretty girl!' said Flora; 'do you suppose that the people who sit to artists are really as lovely as they are painted?'

'I imagine,' replied Lord Lillebonne, 'that artists correct any defects which they may find in their models. But a clever portrait-painter will manage to preserve the likeness while correcting the defects. I should think that the model who sat for this picture was an extremely pretty girl.'

He read and re-read the entry in the catalogue—'Apple Blossoms' . . . Felix Vereker.' He did not know the name of Vereker as a painter, so he turned to the list of exhibitors, and found, 'Vereker, Felix, Willow Green Studios.' But he did not know where Willow Green might be.

' I should just like to ask the price of this picture,' he said to Flora, as he looked round for some one of whom to inquire.

A young man of clerkly aspect sat at a small table with piles of catalogues and written papers before him. When Lille-bonne inquired the price of ' Apple Blos-soms,' the young man took up a catalogue in which appeared the price of every picture, jotted down in pencil. He turned over the pages until he came to what he was seeking, and then he said, 'Twenty pounds,' in a very contemptuous voice; for how could a clerk respect a painter who only priced his picture at twenty pounds?

'I should like to buy it,' said Lord Lillebonne; 'at least, if the artist cares to sell it.'

'Artists are generally glad to sell their pictures,' said the young man, making a cabalistic mark in the catalogue; 'you will have to give your name and pay down half the price.'

Now the earl had not ten pounds in his pocket; he grew red and fidgety, and stammered out,

'I have no money with me, except a

few shillings ; perhaps I could speak to Mr. Vereker.'

The clerk shrugged his shoulders and looked about the room, which was clearing a good deal as the tea-hour approached ; not seeing Vereker, he went up on the short flight of marble stairs towards the upper gallery, but on them he met Vereker, who was growing tired of the crowd and thinking of getting out into the air.

'There's an old fellow wanting to buy your "Apple Blossoms," but he has no money with him. You had better come and speak to him.'

Felix followed the clerk to the table, and as soon as he saw Lady Flora he felt that here was a girl of whom he could paint a picture even prettier than that which he was about to sell.

Lord Lillebonne was fingering his shaggy grey moustache.

'Oh, Mr. Vereker, I beg your pardon, but if you would allow me I should be very glad to possess your "Apple Blossoms."'

'I shall be only too happy to sell it,' answered Vereker; 'I think I am speaking to Lord Lillebonne?'

'Yes. I am much pleased with the little picture; it is very pretty. Unfortunately, I have neither money nor cheque with me;' he was rubbing one thin hand over the other with a nervous action, and his white face had taken a flush of shame.

'It is of no consequence whatever,' said Vereker; then turning to the clerk he added, 'please mark my picture as sold to Lord Lillebonne.'

' Thank you, thank you,' said the earl, apparently much relieved; 'here is my card,' which he fumbled out of an old card-case; ' and, perhaps, Mr. Vereker, you could make it convenient to call uopn me some morning.'

Felix replied that he should be most happy to do so; and all the time he was talking to the father he took occasional glances at the daughter, seeing in her not only such beauty as he had seen in Edith Crane, but also that stamp of high birth, that *cachet* of nobility, which is seldom wanting in the women of the English aris-tocracy. A duchess is not always beauti-ful, but she generally looks like a duchess.

' A very interesting exhibition,' said Lillebonne, becoming more at his ease with young Vereker, ' very interesting; a good deal of affectation among some of your members, but, on the whole, very interesting. I am very ignorant on the subject, but it certainly appears to me that the knowledge and the love of art are increasing very largely among us.'

Vereker bowed.

Lord Lillebonne went on.

' I remember what passed as art in the days of my childhood. The illustrated books of that period would not now be placed in the hands of the poorest children. The coloured prints which used to please the middle-classes would not now be hung on a costermonger's wall. They still linger in out-of-the-way villages, but only as curiosities, and I would venture to ask, and I am hopeful that some one will contradict me if I am wrong——'

Flora saw that her father was getting into what she called his 'House of Lords manner,' which consisted in rambling on in a drily didactic style, which wearied those who tried to listen to it.

'Father,' she said, softly, 'do you think Mr. Vereker would point out to us some of the best things here?'

'With the greatest pleasure,' cried Felix.

His alacrity alarmed the earl.

'No, my dear, I think your mother and sister must be waiting for us somewhere.'

Glancing round the room he saw that they three were the only occupants of it; even the clerk had retired to some private den.

'I think,' said Vereker, boldly, 'that the rest of your party have gone to the tea-room. Allow me to show you the way.'

Nothing loth, Flora let herself be escorted by the young artist, and her poor father had no choice but to follow; he could not allow her to be carried quite away from him. Arrived at the tea-room, they met a stream of people coming away from it; but still there was a large assemblage of ladies and gentlemen, and a considerable clatter of cups and saucers. The earl caught sight of the purple feathers in his wife's bonnet, and was re-assured.

'Wait here a moment,' said Vereker to Lady Flora, ' and I will bring you some tea.'

He went away, and shortly afterwards returned with tea for both Flora and her father. Then he brought bread-and-butter and cakes; and Lillebonne, who was devoted to afternoon-tea, felt his heart warming towards the young man, who was, moreover, good-looking, gentlemanly, and altogether attractive. It did not strike him—such things never do strike fathers—that perhaps Flora might also find Felix Vereker attractive. He ate his bread-and-butter and drank his tea while Felix discoursed, chiefly on art, Flora listening with both ears. She caught an occasional intonation which sounded like an echo from across the Atlantic, but the sound was not unpleasant; indeed it was very piquant. People streamed away, and the tea-room became half-empty, and still the Lillebonne party were all there, though in two divisions.

'Who is that man talking to your sister?' the earl asked of Flora.

But Flora did not know: a short, squat little fellow, with a parchmenty yellow face, colourless hair and moustache, and yet with a curious twinkle of humour in his pale eyes.

Almost at the same moment, Lady Lillebonne, Clara, and their ugly companion moved towards the door, and the earl, Flora, and Vereker stood up from their seats.

'We really must be going,' said the countess to her husband; 'this is Sir Ronald Stanley. I think you knew his father.'

'Yes, I did,' said Lillebonne, who had no pleasant recollections of the late baronet; 'let me introduce Mr. Vereker.'

Mutual bows, and then a general movement to get away. In the hall Vereker had a few more words with Flora, and Sir Ronald a few more words from Clara.

' You will come in some day to lunch ?' said the countess to Sir Ronald.

' You will call on me some morning ?' said Lillebonne to Vereker.

Then the landau received its occupants, hats were lifted, and the day of the private view was over as far as our special friends were concerned.

CHAPTER V.

THE UNSUCCESSFUL AUTHOR.

That city's atmosphere is dark and dense,
 Although not many exiles wander there,
With many a potent evil influence,
 Each adding poison to the poisoned air ;
Infections of unutterable sadness,
Infections of incalculable madness,
 Infections of incurable despair.
  The City of Dreadful Night. JAMES THOMSON.

A SHABBY slouching figure was tramping up and down a paved bit of pathway which runs for a hundred yards or so beside the Thames near Fulham. Only a low brick wall divides the footway from the water which a high tide washes against the wall. It was an April evening, and the sunset light was strong in the west; an amber glow near the horizon, and above it some level grey clouds which divided it from a space of pure pale green, that green only to be seen in April skies. Higher still were clouds of darker grey deepening into purple, and overhead was an intense azure specked with steady, mellow stars. The shabby figure tramped up and down many times; the head seldom uplifted itself to gaze at the glories above it. Nor did Tothill look once at the black river rippling against the wall. Several times his hand went into his pocket as if to bring out something, but each time it emerged empty. Then at last he began to mutter,

' Dare I do it? Have I the courage, the hardihood? Would there be crime in such a deed? Better men than I have done such things, and the world has cried shame on them, while those who knew their temptations have tenderly pitied them.'

He stood beside the wall and looked over on the river.

' There,' he said, in that theatrical voice with which he often talked to himself, ' there lies a mean by which to escape from my difficulties, but not for me! That which hampers me in the one case also hampers me in the other. Oh, this Republic of Letters! What corruptions exist in every Republic! We republicans, are we better off than the aristocrats? Am I, Augustus Algernon Tothill, one

whit better off than the Earl of Lillebonne? Truly, in worldly matters I am
poorer than he, though in brain and intellect infinitely his superior. But he—proud
wearer of a material coronet—tramples on
me the man of letters, the historian, the
future author of novels which will inau-
gurate a new era of literature. He wal-
lows in his whitebait and champagne in
Eaton Place, while I have come to this!'

Tothill leaned over the parapet of the
wall, a forlorn object stretched headfore-
most towards destruction.

A footstep behind him, a hand on his
shoulder, and he turned his head and saw
Felix Vereker.

'What are you doing here?' said Felix,
sharply.

'Oh—nothing.'

'Come away, old man. Come with me.'

'Why should I? Where are you going?'

'I am going to dinner. Have you dined?'

'Dined? Oh no, I don't think I am hungry.'

'Will you do me a kindness? I can't bear sitting down to dinner alone; just come and talk to me, and cheer me up while I eat.'

'If you wish it,' replied Tothill; and they slowly went away from the river-side.

The amber and green had faded from the sky, the tide had turned, and the water was running down very fast. The red curtains which screened the old bow-window of the little eating-house were bright from the light within. Both men knew that this was the evening for beef-steak puddings.

Vereker said to the maid,

'Bring two beef-steak puddings, and a pint of sherry.' And when they were brought, he said to Tothill, 'Do me the honour to be my guest at dinner.'

The man of letters looked slightly confused, but said nothing, and seated himself, and fell-to on the viands with remarkable vigour. When he had eaten and drank, the haggard look on his face passed away, and a smile took possession of him.

Vereker now ventured to ask him,

'What folly were you thinking of, there by the river?'

'Well, it was folly, worse than folly. For one thing, I was wondering whether one could catch fish here at Fulham, and whether, if one were put to it, one could in that way supply one's bodily craving for material food. But that is not all. Vereker, would you believe it,' and here he lowered his voice, lest he should be overheard, and the tears of shame were in his eyes, ' the thought was in my mind whether I could summon courage to cheat the good people who keep this hospitable house—whether I could come in and eat a dinner, and then tell them that I had no means of paying them.'

Vereker sat silent, but an amused look stole over his countenance; he had suspected poor Tothill of intending suicide while he had only been meditating a petty felony. And then the smile faded away, and Felix became very grave, as he thought how more than sad it was that a man of education and ability should be in such distress. He was young, was Felix Vereker, and he had a hundred a-year private income, and he did not yet understand how heavily handicapped a man is with education and ability and no private income. The poor man with genius is pretty certain to force his way upward; the fire which burns within him will keep him warm, and will heat his frugal meals, until he has attained to a position where clothing and food come as natural events; and the man of ability who has some private income can keep himself going until his talents have won him such a place as he deserves. But education and ability with nothing more create aspirations and hopes which they have not the force to make realities, and the man starves before he can achieve that small success which is to be his ultimate reward.

' Letters are not a very paying profession,' said Vereker.

' Not to some of us. But when I hear of the enormous sums paid by those rascally publishers for rubbish—some sensational story—some ridiculous pantomime play—some silly weak verse—I feel how blind they are to their own interests——'

' And to yours,' added Vereker.

Augustus Tothill gave a burst of laughter which made the diners at other tables turn and stare. The clerks and shopmen who came hither for supper knew that

Tothill was a *hauthor* and Vereker a *hartist*, and this peal of merriment sounded to them like the laughter of the gods.

'Fill your pipe,' said Felix, handing his tobacco to his companion; 'tell me, has not the *Monday Moon* been giving her proper light of late?'

'She is only a crescent, and but few rays of silver enlighten my darkness. Oh, they pay shamefully—absolutely only a penny a line. Then again, the *Advance Magazine* says it will print a paper of mine in the first number, but they can't pay their contributors at present. The more one wants money the more one can't get it. If I were a Rider Haggard, or a Besant, or even a Mrs. Humphrey Ward, the publishers would be outbidding each other for my writings.   The world is full of injustice, and the greatest of all injustice is that done to authors.'

' But what made you take to writing at first, Tothill ?'

' The love of it.   I began to write when I was seven years old.   My father was the master of a National School, and I had books at my disposal.   So I read, and then I wrote.   My father died mad—he drank.'

After a pause Vereker said,

' When did you begin to publish ?'

Tothill recovered himself.

' When a mere lad.   I sent some sketches of village life to a magazine, and the editor said he would print them though he could not afford to pay for them.   As I was still kept by my father, and was supposed to be preparing to be a schoolmaster, I was en-

chanted at appearing in print. All my
work went to that magazine, but I never
got a penny for it. Then I heard of a new
review about to be started and to pay a
guinea a page. They took my papers; I
left my mother, now a widow, and gave
myself up to writing. After six numbers
the new review collapsed, and I got no
guineas. Since then, some seventeen
years, I scramble along somehow. But
the day will come when you will be proud
to know me, and when I will return this
dinner with one of whitebait, venison,
turtle-soup, oyster-patties, chartreuse and
champagne, I will !'

Vereker laughed, and said,

' I hold you to that promise. But don't
you sometimes come across generous
publishers ?'

'Never; I don't expect generous publishers; why should they be generous?
They would be great fools if they were.   I
only want them to be just.   Now, I'll tell
you what a certain firm did to me : a high
class firm, established a hundred-and-fifty
years, much given to bringing out religious
literature.   They commissioned me to write
a little work on a certain period of Spanish
history—you may have seen the book—it
deals with Ferdinand and Isabella, and
that lot; I had to buy and hire any number of books, and the story itself took me
three months of hard labour.   After I had
begun they sent me a letter to ask what
price I expected ; I thought it best to be
moderate, and I said thirty pounds.   They
wrote that they could not give more than
twenty pounds, but if I consented to that

price they would send an agreement for me to sign.   My poverty and not my will consented.'

' If you consented, what complaint have you against them ?'

' Hear me out.   The agreement arrived ; it declared that they agreed to give me twenty pounds for the copyright of my tale—that is to say, fifteen pounds on publication of the first edition, and five pounds more if it went into a second edition.'

Vereker said,

' Has it gone into a second edition ?'

' Not that I know of.'

' It was a pity that you signed the agreement.'

' I was young, I was hungry; *que voulez-vous* ?'

Then for a time the two men sat

silent and smoked; Vereker had had experience of some of the ways of picture-dealers, but he saw that there are publishers who also knew how to drive hard bargains. And he thought that painters lead pleasanter lives than authors. The man who writes is a lonely being, and the woman who writes is even lonelier; he—or she—may sit all day in some little dull room, the back bent, the fingers cramped, over sheets of paper and penny bottles of ink; the manuscript may be sent off by post, the proofs arrive by post, the whole business of publication be transacted by post, and the solitary worker never comes face to face with editor, or with publisher, or with any fellow-author. The appearance, the age, the sex even, of the writer may remain entirely unknown to publisher and to public; and the pen which delights a hundred thousand readers may be to its owner as the crutch of an agonized body or as the sword of a self-destroying soul.

But the painter, if he studies nature, sits out in the open air, he drinks in sunshine and light, the country people wonder at him, the passers-by stop and admire and say a pleasant word; if he studies human nature, he has the society of noble men and beautiful women. A Lord Lillebonne and a Lady Flora Vere de Vere may be among his acquaintances, perhaps even among his friends.

'I would not change with you,' said Vereker at length, a strange light in his eyes, and a strange softness in his voice;

'I think the painter is happier than the author.'

Tothill took up this remark as a challenge. His spirits had revived, and he proceeded to show eloquently.how great are the enjoyments of literary life; how the author increases his own fund of knowledge as he increases that of his readers; how he lives among his characters who are to him far more real than the people amid whom he dwells. He can paint the woman whom he loves so that all other men must love her though they have never seen her; and he can caricature the man whom he hates so that the whole world shall detest and abhor the life-like yet loathsome presentment.

'I could hold that Earl of Lillebonne,' snarled Tothill, who never having been acquainted with men of rank always gave them their full titles, 'up to universal execration; I could ferret out his terrific secret and place it in the glare of the midday sun.'

'What can you mean?' exclaimed Felix, astonished and alarmed.

'He is a proud, surly cur!' cried the author, bringing his fist down on the oil-cloth covered round table; 'I saw the scorn on his sickly face; and I will pay him out. Had he spoken civilly to me, had he offered to help me in my profession, then I would have treated him well; I would have dedicated a book to him. As it is I will never rest until I have discovered the family skeleton, and I will drag it out from its cupboard, and display it to the world. The *Daily Photograph* would pay well for such a paper; and if I could get on the staff of the *Daily Photograph* my fortune would be made.'

It had often crossed Felix Vereker's mind that his poor friend Augustus Tothill was not quite sane. This extraordinary outburst of rage against a man who had committed no offence, and this fury of desire to hunt out the 'family skeleton' of the Vere de Veres, seemed to Felix to savour of madness, though there was method in the plan for getting on the staff of the *Daily Photograph*.

'How has Lord Lillebonne offended you? And, by-the-by, he pronounces his name not Lilebon, but *Lillybun*.'

'He cut short my explanations at the Advance the other day in the most beastly manner; and why can't he pronounce his name as it is spelt?'

'Really! And what do you know about the family secret?'

'I don't know anything,' said Tothill, 'except that there is one. Surely you must know about it.'

'I have never even heard of it. You must remember that I have only been three years in England, and those three years have been almost entirely occupied in studying art.'

'Then I will tell you what is known. The Earl of Lillebonne has two country seats—think of it—that semi-idiot with two large places, and myself with a garret! And at one of those houses—I don't know which, but I can find out easily enough—there is a secret room which is never opened but on the day on which the eldest son comes of age. On that day the reigning earl takes his eldest son, who is called by courtesy the Viscount Senlac, into the secret room, and when that viscount comes out, he is a wiser and a sadder man, and he is never seen to smile again.'

' A strange legend,' said Vereker.

' Legend, man! it is a fact. I noticed myself how nervous and queer the old earl was the other day. I don't believe he smiled even at the Pag's get-up. Now, I am going to find out what is in that secret chamber. The records of a ghastly murder, or—or—something horrible.'

' Better leave it alone,' said Vereker.

' I won't leave it alone!' cried Tothill,

excitedly, ' do you suppose that when one sees a chance of copy of the sensational kind, that one is to let it slip from one's grasp?'

At this moment the master of the eating-house stalked through the hot, smoke-filled room, and turned out all the gas-burners save one. Slowly the guests rose; those who had not paid their scores, laid down money on the tables; they all got into their overcoats, and trooped out into the cool night. Tothill seized Vereker's arm, and continued to pour out abuse of Lord Lillebonne.

It seemed to Felix that his poor friend was not sane, and he wondered whether the sherry—of which Tothill had drunk nearly the whole—had affected a brain weakened by constant want of nourishing food. Then he thought of heredity, and that perhaps the drunken father had bequeathed a diseased brain to his son ; and he thought of the dark, gloomy republic, of which Tothill was a starving citizen, the golden possibilities, the squalid realities, the miserable disappointments, the promptings of despair.

They came near to Willow Green.

' Go home now, Tothill, and sleep soundly, and don't trouble yourself about Lord Lillebonne. His family secret is nothing to you. Take up pleasanter subjects for your pen.'

' I must take up what will pay best.'

Tothill gave a yell of laughter and disappeared in the darkness. Vereker went on to the red-brick house and let himself in with his latch-key. He did not turn into the studio, but went straight to his bed-room; for possibly Coleman might be in the studio, and on this evening Vereker did not wish to have to talk to Coleman.

This young man, Felix Vereker, had a habit not very usual with young men, especially those who live on the confines of Bohemia; a habit of reading every night in an old book translated from the Hebrew and the Greek. He did so this evening, and afterwards he knelt upon the floor, with his hands clasped together. When he stood up he began slowly to undress, and, as he wound his watch and took off his ring, he thought very sadly of Augustus Tothill and his life. Little could he, or anyone, do to help the unsuccessful author; there is no back stairs to literary fame. But perhaps Tothill

could be prevented from annoying Lord
Lillebonne. Any endeavour to pry into
the family secret—if secret there were—
must be extremely distasteful to the earl.
And Felix went on to reason that, if Tothill made himself objectionable to Lord
Lillebonne, the peer would be sure to
include Vereker in his displeasure, as
being a friend of the half-insane writer.

As Felix pulled off his collar, his mind
had strayed away to Lady Flora de Vere;
it had often strayed to her since that day
at the Advance. He had not yet been to
call on the earl; why not? Some inde-
finable feeling of shyness held him back.
He did not want to seem anxious to keep
up the acquaintance of an earl. Had it
been a poor man and his daughter who
were in question, Felix would have gone

to see them long ago ; but a peer—no, no
tuft-hunting, nor the appearance of such
a thing. And yet, to hold off too long
would be foolish and ungentlemanly.
Lord Lillebonne's friendly request should
be met in a friendly manner. And Felix
was not above hoping for a commission ;
already he had begun a head of Edith
Crane's sister, little Nellie ; and he had
been planning other work which might
please the earl, or some of the earl's rich
friends. Yes, the very next morning he
would pay his visit in Eaton Place. And
if he should chance to meet Lady Flora—
well, she would not eat him up, and probably no harm would come of it. A girl
whom he had seen once—did he think
himself a perfect fool? And, though
she was the daughter of an English

peer, is not an American citizen——?

Felix fell asleep, thinking, not of the English peer and his daughter, but of that unfortunate citizen of the republic of letters who was determined to bring shame on the English peer. And, our dreams seldom being suggested by our thoughts, he dreamed of painting Lady Flora's portrait, and of being wonderfully successful, and of enjoying the task as he had never before enjoyed any task; for this was indeed a labour of love. And then he awoke, with a jerk and a start, and muttered,

' A dream—perhaps only a dream !'

CHAPTER VI.

BELGRAVIA AND BOHEMIA.

Out upon it, I have loved
Three whole days together ;
And am like to love three more
If it prove fine weather.
                    SIR JOHN SUCKLING.

THE greatest charm of the English climate
is its uncertainty. However disagreeable
it may be to-day, a change is certainly
near. It snows hard with a cutting wind,
but last week the land was wrapped in a
still, wet fog, and next week the sun will
shine fiercely and the dust lie thick on

our boots. The 15th of July and the 15th of December, 1892, were exactly alike in London as to temperature and duration of sunshine. How many variations there must have been between those two days! Monotony is the most wearisome thing in life; and there is no monotony in the English climate. For which we should be very thankful.

It is a glorious day in early May; high summer in London. The squares have green hedges and green trees; in the parks there are beds full of glowing and delicious flowers; every balcony, every window-sill in the fashionable quarters are ablaze with marguerites, calceolaria, geraniums, lobelia, and other flowers, set out daintily and artistically about the fronts of those stolid houses which have no possibility of beauty except floral decoration. But stop—may there not be human decoration?

An awning is spread over the balcony of Lord Lillebonne's house in Eaton Place; an awning striped red and white, and somehow reviving memories of boats plying between Bellaggio and Menaggio. And never did a sunnier day shine on Lake Como than that which now shines upon Belgravia.

Felix Vereker descends from the top of an omnibus and walks down Sloane Street. He presently turns to the left, and makes his way to Eaton Place, somewhat undecided in his course, because he is not much at home in the haunts of the wealthier classes. It must be confessed that he has a little 'got himself up' for this morning's visit. He wears a new pale grey scarf, his hat has been carefully brushed, his umbrella tightly rolled, his boots blacked by his own hands, with some wonderful composition which Coleman lauds highly. Now, Vereker is not a man to think about his dress as a means of softening the heart of one of his fellow-men ; what, then, can be the reason of all this care spent to-day on his toilette ?

He arrives at the west end of Eaton Place. He looks up and down the street, scanning the numbers on the doors. He soon sees that which he seeks, and he slowly approaches it. Over the whole of the balcony, which includes the square top of the porch, extends an awning, and from under it peep out lovely, bright flowers. A few moments Vereker lingers, glancing at the flowers and at the awning. He fancies that in the shadows he sees forms moving; figures clothed in white, or blue, or mauve, graceful female figures.

He steps up on a marble-paved door-step, and knocks with the heavy knocker. Had it been after three o'clock, a couple of footmen with a butler in reserve would have responded to his peal; as it was only just eleven o'clock, one young man in un-dress livery opened the door after a few minutes' delay.

'Is Lord Lillebonne at home?' Felix asked.

'I think his lordship is within,' replied the footman, showing Felix into a small morning-room off the hall. Some needle-work lay on a table, betokening the recent presence of a lady.

The footman went away, and presently returned, saying, 'Will you please to walk into his lordship's study.'

This study was at the back of the morning-room, and looked into a sort of yard which lay between Lord Lillebonne's house and his stables. A few struggling lilac-bushes bordered a gravel-path which led from the house to the stables. The look-out was dull, but the room itself was extremely cheerful. Many small but fine pictures hung on the walls. Between the pictures were bookshelves filled with richly-bound volumes of which Felix caught some of the titles, such as *Shakespeare's Works, Milton's Works, Byron's Works, Waverley Novels*. There was a time-piece which looked very ancient; a pair of bronze horses, antique as Felix could

see ; and two or three bits of old blue
china.

Lord Lillebonne was in his dressing-
gown, a rich brown plush trimmed with
gold cord; and this dress seemed more
congruous to the pale and thin elderly
man than the lighter and tighter attire of
society. He seemed more at home in it,
and Vereker immediately felt more at
home with him.

The artist had sent in his card, and the
earl was ready to receive him.

' Oh, Mr. Vereker, this is very good of
you. I am afraid I am occupying your
valuable time.'

' Not at all, my lord. One cannot always be at work; and this fine morning it
has been very pleasant to come out into
the open air.'

'Yes, it is very fine. Won't you sit down? There is an armchair somewhere. Yes, it is very good of you ; very good.'

Lord Lillebonne was pulling about the papers on his writing-table, and had the nervous, fidgetty manner usual with him. An awkward silence followed, which Vereker thought that he ought not to be the first to break ; but, when it became oppressive, he said,

'Allow me to remark that you have some very fine pictures.'

'Oh, yes,' cried the earl, brightening ; 'yes, truly. That Cuyp is considered quite a masterpiece; the sunshine in it is wonderful. I often look from it to the window to see if the sun is really shining. And that Metsu, over there. Is it not a gem? Did you ever see such minute details? Oh, wonderful, wonderful!'

'Is this a Guido?' enquired Felix, who was coasting round the room; 'I fancy I must have seen it when I was studying in Florence.'

'You are right, Mr. Vereker; you may have seen it in Florence, or a replica of it, or a copy. I think there can be no reasonable doubt that this is the genuine original, and the picture at Florence a good copy. Those Italian fellows are wonderfully clever at copying.'

'They are,' returned Felix; 'at Venice I saw a man in the *Belle Arti* whose copies were identical with the originals. He had the same rich colouring, and his Bonifacios and Carpaccios were equal to the originals; but he could do nothing more than copy. He could not have painted from the life, not to save his. Now, you know, the man was not an artist.'

Vereker's tone had become very familiar, carried away as he was by his subject; the earl was slightly surprised at it, but the bright, good-looking young man was a pleasant companion, and for the moment Lillebonne forgot the difference in their position, forgot his nervousness, forgot himself in fact, and was friendly and chatty. Vereker's genuine admiration of the fine paintings in the study opened the heart of the reserved man.

' I have a Holbein in the dining-room,' said his lordship, ' and two Romneys; also a Reynolds and a Gainsborough, all four are family portraits. And in the drawing-rooms there are some good miniatures.'

' Miniatures are most interesting,' remarked Felix, thinking of the female figure which had flitted under that red and white striped awning; 'the art of miniature painting has almost died out in our day; photography has taken, but not filled, its place.'

'Very true,' returned the peer; 'I believe my lady is in the drawing-room, or we might go and look at the miniatures. I think I hear my youngest daughter playing the piano. So we must be content to sit here without seeing them.'

'Them!' thought Felix, 'the ladies, or the miniatures?' He said aloud, 'I have one miniature which I value highly, and only one. It is also a family portrait.'

Lord Lillebonne mused over that sentence of Vereker's. Could an American have ancestors, or family portraits? Could

a portrait-painter, a mere portrait-painter,
have ancestors and family portraits ?   The
earl was somewhat old-fashioned in his
ideas ; he still kept a haunting notion that
men of good family only went into the Guards,
or the Foreign Office, or the Navy, and that
portrait-painting was quite a Bohemian,
not to say plebeian occupation.   Of course
it was true that artists were sometimes
made baronets ; but he only knew one man
of old and noble descent who had adopted
portrait-painting as a profession ; and
Lillebonne forgave him that lapse because
he was such a very bad painter.

'Our family is English,' Felix was
saying.

'I suppose most American families are
English.   We are all cousins, no doubt.
And Vereker is a good English name.'

There was just a something in Lord
Lillebonne's tones which nettled the young
man. But then, the peer had a lovely
daughter, and Felix felt constrained to forgive him. At this moment he heard a door
open and shut, and then he saw Lady
Flora, in a ravishing light blue gown, pass
out into that gloomy garden, accompanied
by a great collie, and enter a door in the
stable-wall, and so disappear. He looked
after her in her rapid transit.

'My daughter is going to visit her favourite horse,' said Lillebonne, who had
noticed a curious look in Vereker's eye,
though he did not know what it meant; 'I
suppose you do not paint horses?'

'I am sorry to say I cannot paint
animals.'

'Flora looks very well in her habit,'

said the earl, thoughtfully; ' and that brings me to what I really want to propose to you, Mr. Vereker; I dare say you know that I have bought the " Apple Blossoms." '

Yes, Felix knew it.

' And it struck me the other day that my daughter would paint quite as well as your model.'

Felix had no breath with which to speak ; he coloured and bowed.

' Lady Flora has much the same complexion and hair as the girl in your picture, with, I venture to think, something added.'

' A great deal added,' said Felix, in a low tone.

' And if you would undertake the work——'

' There is nothing,' cried the artist,

'which I would undertake so willingly.'

'But the scheme must remain a strict secret. Lady Lillebonne's birthday is in July, and I should greatly like to surprise her with a present of the portrait of her younger daughter. We have several likenesses of Lady Clara, but not one good one of Lady Flora. Therefore, if she sits to you, the sittings and the portrait must remain a secret until the day when I present the picture to my wife.'

Felix thought that this would be the most excellent arrangement, but he restrained all expressions of delight lest he should betray himself.

'Lady Flora would have to sit in your studio, and I should come with her myself or send her maid with her. And, before quite settling the matter, I should wish, with your permission, to visit your studio.'

'Oh, certainly,' said Felix; 'whenever you like to come I shall be very happy to see you.'

Vereker's tone rather grated on the earl's ear; there was a certain confidence in it, confidence in his own power and his own position, which Lillebonne hardly expected to find in a struggling artist.

'I will come some morning, shortly; and now, as you are willing to undertake the commission, I need not further occupy your time.'

Felix got towards the door.

'Willow Green is——?' queried the earl.

Felix described how it could be found.

'Thank you; I daresay a cabman will be able to find it. Good-morning.'

And Felix shortly was out in the street. He looked up at the awning, which had lost its charm, for Lady Flora was in the stables. He got into the Park and walked among the bushes, and into Kensington Gardens. He was naturally much excited. A commission to paint a beautiful girl, the daughter of an earl! that alone was enough excitement for a young artist. And when it is remembered that the girl's beauty and manners had struck the artist far more than her rank, it will be understood how very much excited he needs must be.

He was also somewhat annoyed and angry. Lord Lillebonne had put on airs of haughtiness and grandeur which an American could hardly endure; indeed, had not the earl been Lady Flora's father,

Felix Vereker would not have endured them. Did the mere accidents of rank and wealth make one man superior to another? Lillebonne, with his almost imbecile nervousness and his idiotic assumption of the part of a *connoisseur*, placed him far below a man like Vereker, who understood art practically. Suppose the artist should turn, like the proverbial worm, and refuse to paint the peer's daughter? At this thought, Vereker laughed and shook his head.

Then arose the question of terms. Felix ought to be well paid by the head of the caste of Vere de Vere. Fifty pounds? Yes, perhaps it would not be advisable to ask a higher price; indeed, if the earl should haggle at that sum, Felix would say forty, thirty, twenty.

Now that he was engaged to paint Lady Flora, he must do it at any price, or any loss; for it would be a labour not of lucre but of love.

How delightful it would be to have her sitting in his studio! to be able to study her sweet face, and her angelic expression. A man would be the better for the society of so charming a woman. Already, after one afternoon with her, and one passing glimpse of her, he found that he could think of little else than her eyes, her voice, her hand. Of course it was utterly absurd, nothing could come of it; earls' daughters do not marry penniless American artists; but a wise man enjoys the passing pleasures which are sent to him; and Felix Vereker was a wise man, and quite ready to fall desperately in love with

Lady Flora Vere de Vere. As for the future, even if matters went to the extremest point, and he should find his happiness dependent on Flora, and Flora should confess that her happiness was dependent on him, what then? Was there any just impediment?

CHAPTER VII.

THE INVALID FATHER.

I know my life's a pain, and but a span ;
 I know my sense is mocked in everything :
And, to conclude, I know myself a man,
 Which is a proud and yet a wretched thing.
 Nosce Teipsum. Sir John Davies (1570--1626).

THE work with which Felix Vereker was playing since he had finished the ' Apple Blossoms ' had all along very little interest for him; Nellie Crane was a pretty child enough, not so fair nor so brightly coloured as her sister, but with a certain gracefulness which made her valuable as a model. She was a patient little thing, and would sit silent for hours while Vereker worked very lazily, smoked, and spoke little. Sometimes Edith came with the child as far as the door of the studios; but more often Nellie came alone. The extreme quietness of his young model struck Felix as unnatural in a girl of eleven, but with the carelessness of a young man he took little notice of it, and supposed it to be constitutional. He painted mechanically, and felt that he was not doing good work; he thought that he should do better work when he began on Lady Flora's portrait. Nellie Crane—'Buttercups,' as he meant to call the picture—did not inspire him. He even found more pleasure in a full-length reproduction of the 'family miniature,'

which he had mentioned to Lord Lillebonne. At these two pictures he worked
fitfully, and with the feeling upon him
that he was only filling up his time while
waiting for the great event of his life—
the 'Portrait of the Lady Flora Vere de
Vere.'

Not that Felix was in love with Flora;
of course not, when he had only seen her
twice, only spoken to her once; when he
was an unknown artist, and she a fashionable young lady. But it would be a
great gain to the unknown artist to become known as the man who had painted
the portrait of the fashionable young
lady. Oh, Felix knew very well that
he had not fallen in love with Flora;
he had been in love many times, had
conducted many flirtations, was well up

in the art of love-making. His admiration of Lady Flora was quite unlike that which he had felt for any of his former flames. And it was the artist, not the man, who was so very anxious for Flora's sittings to begin.

He had the studio very much to himself at this time; for Coleman had begun to make excursions into the country for studies of nature.

' And I suppose I had better clear out on those days when your grand young lady comes to be painted.'

' Well,' said Vereker, ' perhaps I should get on better if I had the studio to myself. But no day is fixed at present.'

' Let me know the days when they are fixed, and I will make myself scarce. I think I shall do " Eton College " as a match for " Windsor Castle." I hear that there's an alderman who is nibbling at the " Windsor ;" now, aldermen always like things in pairs ! so I shall get an " Eton " ready for him.'

' You are a sharp man of business,' said Vereker.

They were talking together while Felix worked languidly, and Nellie Crane sat silent in the pose which had been chosen for ' Buttercups.'   As they talked they heard Quekett's heavy step coming up the stairs, and then they heard his heavy knock on the door.

Coleman flung it open, and cried, ' Enter Quekett, the porter, with a head !'

He looked round to see whether Nellie was amused; but she did not even smile.

Quekett was panting for breath.

' Them stairs do try me uncommon.'

'Sit down, Quekett; there's no spare chair, but plenty of room on the floor. Do you call the stairs trying? Why, when I was in Paris, studying the French impressionist school, I lived *au septième*; and I have counted eleven storeys to some of the Edinburgh houses. I assure you five storeys is nothing! I could tell you five hundred without any difficulty.'

Still Nellie did not laugh.

'I know, Mr. Coleman,' said Quekett, ' that five floors with near upon a hundred steps is nothing to a young gent like you; but when it's me it's different.'

'Not a bit different, Quekett; the stairs never change. But, pray, to what do we owe the honour of your visit?'

'Well, it was that there little gal that I wanted to speak to. She slips away so sudden-like when Mr. Vereker has done with her, that I says to Mrs. Quekett—leastways, Mrs. Quekett says to me—just run up and catch her afore she leaves the studio.'

' Does Mrs. Quekett want Nellie?' asked Felix.

Quekett nodded.

' You can go at once, Nellie.'

The child slowly moved and got down from the platform.

'We want you to come and eat a bit of dinner with us,' said the porter to the little girl, in a friendly tone; 'it is nigh upon one o'clock, and it strikes me—leastways, Mrs. Quekett—that your dinner-hour will be past before you get home.'

' We don't have no regular dinner-hour,' said Nellie.

'Nor no regular dinner, I'm a-thinking,' said Quekett.

'What?' cried Coleman, turning upon the porter.

Vereker laid down his palette.

'Don't you have regular meals?' he asked of Nellie.

There came a little burst of tears.

'Not so—not so regular as they used to be before father got so ill.'

The three men stood round the child. Harry Coleman put his hand under her sharp little chin and turned up her face.

'Do you mean to say that you don't get enough to eat?'

The tears had been checked.

'Sometimes I should like a little more. Edie says I have a tremendous appetite, but I am sure she has a very small appetite.'

'Can't you see that she ain't half nourished?' cried Quekett; 'can't you see that every day she comes here she is thinner and thinner?'

'I had not noticed it,' said Coleman.

'She is very thin,' said Vereker.

'Anyone with half an eye can see that the child is pretty well starved,' said Quekett, pinching her scraggy arms, 'it was Rosa who pointed it out to me.'

'Only a woman sees these things,' remarked Felix, hunting in his pockets in case there might be a loose shilling anywhere.

'Yes, it is only women as sees these things.'

'I see it,' cried Harry, passionately, 'I

see it! While we have been keeping the little creature here hour after hour for our advantage, she has been ready to faint from hunger. And Edith too? Child, is your father out of work?'

' He's never in work,' she answered, ' he only does odd bits of mending for the neighbours; he has not strength for hard work, and he can't draw the stitches tight now. And when he stoops much he coughs dreadfully. And all he earns has to go for medicines. And then mother does not get much work now, because she can't keep up with the fashions, and parlour-maids are *that* particular no one knows, mother says. And Edic helps all she can; but there's Arthur and Baby to be looked after, and they take up nearly all Edie's time.'

These details of a sad family history were told by Nellie in a quiet, smooth tone which sounded more like the reciting note of a school exercise than the flow of personal sorrow. Children brought up in decent poverty do not complain; they starve and sicken and die.

'Well, now, come along; we don't want no more talk; there's something else for your mouth to do. There's hand-and-spring of pork, and carrots and mashed potatoes. So come along, Nellie.'

Quekett hurried the child down the stairs, at the bottom of which his Rosa was muttering reproaches for his long delay.

Neither Vereker nor Coleman said anything until the porter and the child were gone, and then they looked at each other with a long, thoughtful gaze.

'I ordered lamb cutlets with tomato sauce for my lunch,' said Felix, 'and I daresay they are served in the dining-hall by this time.'

'And I ordered sweetbread with gooseberry tart to follow—all on the strength of the alderman's possible purchase of "Windsor." We must eat what we have ordered—or shall we send the cutlets and sweetbread to poor Crane?'

'After all, one must eat, even though others are hungry. But I am sorry to hear all this; Crane must be much worse than he used to be. And to think that they do not get enough food!'

Harry washed his brushes with angry energy, and then he went down to the dining-hall common to all the residents in the studios, and saw on a table the covered plates which concealed the food prepared by Mrs. Quekett for himself and Vereker. Two lady students, grotesquely plain and hideously attired, were eating their lunch which consisted of plum cake and tea. When Felix looked at his cutlet he felt that charity begins at home, and that if he wanted to feed the hungry he must feed himself. Which he did. Harry put on an extra plate a portion of the sweetbread, intending to take it to poor Crane. But presently he reflected that sweetbread is a very awkward thing to carry as a brown-paper parcel, that perhaps Crane might not like sweetbread, and that a little money would really be more useful to him. Thus, common-sense prevailed, and he ate his lunch and was thankful for it.

'I really will do something for Crane as soon as Lord Lillebonne has paid for "Apple Blossoms." The gallery closes on the 15th of June, and then I shall get my twenty pounds minus the commission. I suppose it is a better deed to give money in charity than to pay one's bills.'

Harry did not reply. He had brought down his hat, and it lay beside him while he hastily swallowed his luncheon. Now he took it up, thumped it down on his head, and, saying to Felix 'I am going out,' he went out by the swing-doors of the bar-rack-like dining-hall, and down into the airy entrance hall. Here he waited a few minutes until he heard rising from the basement regions the rasping voice of Mrs. Quekett, bidding Nellie run home and not stop to gossip by the way with any other girls, but to carry the little pies safe and not finger them, and stand over her father ever till he had eaten them. Nellie's small clear voice was just audible in some reply of thanks, and then she appeared at the top of the stairs.

She made a curtsey to Coleman, which struck him as old-fashioned but pretty, and then she went out into the street. He was beside her in a moment.

'Nellie, I am going to walk home with you, and to pay a visit to your mother.'

'Oh, thank you, Mr. Coleman,' the child replied, with pleased surprise.

'I have never been in your house, you know, but your sister has told me where you live.'

'It is not a pretty street,' said Nellie; 'and the people who live in it are not very nice people. There are two publics at the corners, and one in the middle ; and there are a great many tipsy people at night. There is a man in our house who is almost always tipsy ; and one day he was *so* rude to Edith.'

' The brute !' exclaimed Harry.

' And he has fights with his wife ; she does not drink, but she *does* swear !   And we all think that some day they will kill each other.'

' And a good thing too !' said Harry, cheerfully.

But his heart was hot and angry at the thought of Edith Crane among scenes of obscenity, drunkenness, and violence. So, too, he was shocked by the knowledge that Edith often wanted food. Of course he knew that superannuated postmen have small pensions, and that broken-down needlewomen must sing 'The song of the shirt;' but it filled him with horror to think that Edith, young, fair, and amiable, should have to share the fate of her parents. He said little more to Nellie; and presently they passed the two public-houses, and turned into the poor, ugly street where lived the Crane family.

Nellie led him up a creaking staircase to the top storey where she dwelt. The roof sloped, and the space was small, but this part of the house was airy and clean. Nellie opened the door of the front-room and entered quickly; Harry took off his hat and entered too.

He saw the ex-postman sitting in an old easy-chair beside the grate in which burnt a little bit of fire; a kettle lay inside the fender; Mr. Crane poked at the embers with an old walking-stick. He saw the dressmaker, faded but pretty, sewing hard at some black material, and every now and then casting an anxious look at her husband or at the baby which lay on a ragged blanket on the floor; she had the long, slender fingers, and the curled-back thumbs of the needle-woman; she stooped, and often closed her eyes as if they ached. He saw Edith standing at a side-table, her sleeves rolled up from her smooth white arms, and with a tub full of linen and soapsuds before her. Her hair was thrown loosely back from her face; exertion and heat had given her a colour, and she looked brilliant, even beautiful in Coleman's eyes, as she paused in her washing and glanced up at him.

He should have bestowed his first greeting on Mrs. Crane, but instead of doing so he rushed at Edith and seized her soapy hands. When he found his all wet and slippery he began to laugh, at which everyone else laughed, even the pale, red-eyed baby.

'Excuse me, Mrs. Crane,' said Coleman, turning to the mother, 'I should have spoken first to you, but then you see I know your daughters. My name is Coleman, Harry Coleman, and I live in the same house with Mr. Vercker to whom your daughters have been sitting.'

'We are much obliged for your visit, sir,' said Mrs. Crane, ' excuse me if I go on with my sewing ; this body is wanted very particular.'

'Pray don't stop for me,' said Harry ;

'I'm a working-man myself, and I know how precious the daylight is.'

'Are you an artist, too, sir, the same as Mr. Vereker?'

'Yes; I am a landscape painter. I'm a poor man now, but I hope one of these fine days to get to one of the upper branches, even if I don't get quite to the top of the tree.'

He perceived that his visit had not disturbed the occupations of the Crane family; the mother sewed, the daughter washed, the father poked the fire. By this time Nellie had opened a parcel and taken out four small pies, one of which she placed before her father, the other three near her mother.

'Now, daddy,' she was saying in her low, refined voice, 'these are mutton-pies which Mrs. Quekett made on purpose for you; and you have got to eat one of them this very minute, sir, do you hear?'

The invalid had brightened up, and was gazing greedily at the food which Nellie placed before him on a broken plate.

' I'll cut it up for you, dear; there, now eat it up quick.'

Crane took a mouthful on his fork eagerly, and put it into his mouth. He chewed it for a long time, and swallowed it with an effort. Then he laid down the fork and pushed away the plate.

' Can't you eat any more?' asked his wife.

He shook his head.

' No appetite, Mr. Crane?' said Harry.

' None at all, sir; and I don't expect to have any till I have had change of air.

As soon as I am strong enough to bear the journey, I am to go to the sea-side, and then I expect my appetite will return. I should be well enough, if only I were a little stronger.'

' I am afraid,' said Harry, ' that you have found the winter very trying?'

' Oh, very trying; and now the warm weather takes every bit of strength out of me. I'm looking forward to the sea, for I know it will do wonders for me. And then, as soon as I come back from the sea, I can get to work again; and if I have more work and more money I shall be able to have food more to my liking.'

' You'll have your tea presently,' said Mrs. Crane ; ' you always enjoy your tea.'

Harry looked at her.

'Tea is not very nourishing.'

'But if he won't take anything else?'

'I would take other things if you brought me what I like. I could eat a bit of the breast of chicken, or oysters; I love oysters.'

'Well, you see, Mr. Crane,' Harry put in, 'oysters are not in season just now. And I believe chickens are very dear in the spring.'

'Of course, that is the way. Whatever would get up my strength and set me up is just the very thing I can't have. Why, I've heard about lap-dogs having roast chickens for their dinner.'

Mrs. Crane cut off a loose thread.

'Yes; when I was in service I saw it with my own eyes. I was young ladies'

maid in the family of the Earl of Lillebonne, and Lady Gertrude, that is the
present earl's sister, used to give chicken
to her dog, a little, yelping, snapping,
thing as ever I saw.'

'Oh,' said Coleman, ' really?   Were
you in the family of the Earl of Lillebonne?'

'I was only with them three months.
But I never could master the hair-dress-
ing; so I had to go in the nursery afterwards; and then I married Crane, and
he thought he should get on in the Post
Office.   But they treated him very badly,
and he never rose at all: and then, when
he got ill, and I had all the children to
look after——'

She broke off with a deep, hopeless
sigh.

' We've buried five,' said the father.

And then Coleman understood that there was strumous disease among the Crane family, and that the father was dying of consumption, which would probably, in some form or another, carry off all the remaining children. The bright colouring of Edith and Nellie, the flabby pallor of the baby, both pointed to the latent constitutional terror. Edith was doomed.

Poor Crane took up again his string of grievances. Harry appeared to listen to them, but he was really engaged in watching the others of the family. Edith had finished her washing ; she wrung out the garments and carried them from the room.

Her mother called out,

'Are you not going to hang them up?'

'Yes,' said Edith from the door; 'I've stretched the line in my room, because I don't think it is good for father to hang the damp things here.'

'She's that thoughtful!' said Mrs. Crane.

After a few minutes, during which no one spoke, Edith returned from the room which she and Nellie occupied; her hair was smoothed, her sleeves were brought down to her wrists, and her brilliant colour had faded. She now looked tired, and sat down on the floor beside the baby. It seemed to Coleman that he must bring his visit to a close.

'I think I must be going,' he said, as he rose; 'but before I go I should like to arrange to keep an engagement made some time ago. Miss Edith promised to come out on the river when the weather grew warm; and now the weather has grown warm.'

Edith rose from the floor. Her colour had come back, her eyes glittered.

'If Miss Edith and Nellie will come with me——'

'It would do me good,' said Mr. Crane, striking the stick on the floor; 'the river comes up from the sea with the tide, and it brings the sea-air with it. Thank you, Mr. Coleman; we accept.'

Harry was in a dilemma; he must take Joseph Crane on the Thames to his own great annoyance, or he must decline to do so, and so offend the father of the girl whom he was learning to love. As wise men do in such dilemmas, he temporised.

' Much will depend on the weather. We could not go out in rain, and you, Mr. Crane, must not go out even if the air be damp. I think I must leave it in this way. When there comes quite a suitable day I will call for you.'

' A Sunday,' said Mrs. Crane.

' Oh, a Sunday, yes.'

' We could not give up any other day,' said Edith, ' because we have so much to do on week-days.'

' A Sunday be it,' returned the yonng man.

And then he shook hands all round, and departed.

Now, as he walked about this monotonous neighbourhood, his thoughts were very various. He was falling in love

with Edith Crane, and he had no intention
of doing anything to break his fall. He
intended, vaguely, to marry her some day,
and in the meantime the courting would
be very pleasant. He knew that she came
of a consumptive family, and that she
ought not to marry; he knew that she was
penniless, and had sickly relatives dragging upon her; he knew that she was not
his social equal, and that the gap between
his father, a small country grocer, and her
father, a letter-carrier, was immeasurable.
He also knew that he had no income
worth speaking of, only occasional wind-
falls from the sale of pictures; he knew
that he owed money all round, to his
tailor, his hatter, his hosier, his colour-
man; he knew that he had no right to
think of marrying a wife unless she were

a woman with money. But, though he knew all these things, he was determined to take Edith Crane out on the river some fine Sunday, and to give her to understand that he was her lover. Moreover, he was determined that Joseph Crane should not be of the party, nor Mrs. Crane, nor the boy Arthur, nor the red-eyed, hideous baby.

No one who is young, or who has been young, shall dare to blame Harry Coleman very severely. 'Love shall still be lord of all,' and shall be so to the end of the chapter. 'The course of true love never did run smooth,' nor ever will to the end of the world. And the love of Harry Coleman and of Edith Crane could prove no exception to the rule. They were sowing the wind and likely to reap the whirlwind, and, in spite of all proverbs and all dehortatory poetry, Harry Coleman was quite resolved to persevere in his love-making, for the girl pleased him very much.

But it was strange that, when he tried to picture her face, he could only see the drawn features of her father. That shrunken figure, huddled in the chair by the fire, came ever before him; that hollow, fretful voice sounded ever in his ears. He thought of Edith as a bride, but Joseph Crane intruded as a corpse; he talked to himself of the marriage service, but he heard the mould flung upon a coffin. He could not, all that day and all that night, shake off the painful impression made upon him by the selfish, whining invalid.

'If only I were a rich man!' sighed Harry, as he turned into a tobacconist's for half a pound of bird's-eye.

CHAPTER VIII.

COMMISSIONS.

Caressés par des fleurs au gai parfum sauvage,
Lavés de la rosée, et s'attardant exprès.
Bonheur. VERLAINE.

THESE two young men, Henry Coleman and Felix Vereker, had now each a secret, not quite known to himself, and not quite unknown to his friend. Each guessed what the other had begun to feel, and each was careful not to betray what he felt or guessed. Felix knew that the lady whom he admired was far above him in rank; Harry knew that the girl whom he loved was far below him in rank. Felix looked on the stammering, nervous, haughty Lord Lillebonne as the greatest impediment to any possible engagement; Harry felt that the querulous, selfish, dying Joseph Crane was the most serious obstacle to the marriage which only obstinate infatuation could think of contracting. The two artists worked together, talked together, dined together, but they never discussed, they seldom even alluded to, Lady Flora Vere de Vere, or Miss Edith Crane.

The first Sunday after Harry's visit to Edith's home was hopelessly wet. He went to call on a friend who lived at Hampstead, and did not go near the Cranes. He had sent Mrs. Crane a postal note for one pound, and was half afraid that she might have discovered from whom it came. As he could not take Edith out, and as the mother might want to thank him, he would not go near them that day. He thought that probably the next Sunday would be fine.

The weather was slow in taking up. It rained all day Monday; and Tuesday was a sunless, steamy day, on which all the rain which had lately fallen tried to rise again towards the skies. On that morning, or rather at that midday, Felix was alone in the studio, Harry having gone to the Academy in order to be able to declare that it contained nothing worth looking at. Vereker was feeling very idle. He had worked for an hour on the full-length reproduction of the family miniature, and then had turned to the 'Butter-cups,' and began painting a hazy land-scape background taken from a sketch which Coleman had lent him. The ances-tress, in her blue gown and gold-spotted gauze scarf, had been turned face to the wall, and Nellie Crane stood unfinished on the easel, when Felix heard a knock on the door.

He shouted 'Come in!' but as no one entered, he sauntered across to interview the visitor. It was Lord Lillebonne.

'Oh, I beg your pardon, my lord!' cried Vereker; 'I thought it would only be one of my set, some art-student. Pray come in and take a seat.'

Lord Lillebonne sat down on a bench covered with an Algerine shawl, both bench and shawl being 'properties' useful in 'interiors.'

'The person who came when I rang,' said the earl, 'was not very courteous; neither can I say that he was very clean.'

'Poor old Quekett has a great deal to do,' said Vereker; 'and he feels the stairs so much that he never comes up them if he can possibly help it.'

'There should be a lift,' said the earl; 'it is hard for your sitters to have to toil up ninety-eight steps.'

'Alas!' said Felix, 'our sitters are so few that we do not trouble ourselves about them.'

'You must have sitters,' said Lord Lillebonne, 'that young girl's head is surely a portrait.'

Felix moved the easel into the best light, and explained that this ' Buttercups ' was own sister to ' Apple Blossoms.' Then he said, rather shyly, that he was glad to know that the latter picture had passed into Lord Lillebonne's possession; and the earl expressed his pleasure at possessing the picture, and seemed to chuckle over his purchase. He quite believed that he had discovered a great genius in this Willow Green studio, and he intended to become the patron of Felix Vereker.

' My coachman had great difficulty in finding this place,' the earl said, with a lofty manner, for the young artist seemed inclined to ignore the differences of rank, and even a genius must be taught that he is not the equal of a peer.

'It is just within the radius,' said Vercker, carelessly.

After some talk, in which Lillebonne
showed that he was not without knowledge of art, though that knowledge was
much less than he supposed, the business
of the day was approached.

'I think,' began the earl, 'that you saw
my daughter, Lady Flora de Vere, the
other day at the Advance Gallery?'

Felix felt a sort of thump at his heart.

'And I think I mentioned that I had
some idea of having her portrait painted?'

'You did, my lord,' replied Felix.

'I should be very glad if you would
undertake the work.'

'I shall be much honoured by the
commission.'

'I intend to present the picture to Lady

Lillebonne as my birthday gift to her, and of course I wish it to be executed in the best possible style. I should not object to its being exhibited in the Academy next year. And you must allow me to add, that a successful likeness of my daughter will bring your name very prominently before the public.'

'That will add profit to pleasure,' said Felix, lightly.

Lord Lillebonne did not quite like that remark; there was something tradesman-like in talking of profit, and something familiar in talking of pleasure. However, one must forgive many things in a genius. And presently it struck Lillebonne that, after all, Vereker wanted to sell his wares, and the price of them must be mentioned.

'Then—as to—terms——'

'Oh, terms be—' Felix caught himself up, '—terms must be as you are pleased to value my work.'

'Well, Mr. Vereker, should you say—fifty pounds?'

'That will suit me capitally. If the picture should not be satisfactory—should not do justice to Lady Flora—I should not allow it to leave my studio.'

Felix thought that it would be very pleasant to keep it there.

At length everything was arranged; Lady Flora would come twice a week, with either her father or her maid, and would sit for an hour or two hours as she might feel inclined. She would wear a dress of some soft green material in which she looked remarkably well, and she would bring some lace or gauze shawl or scarf, in case it should be necessary to soften down the green. The picture must be shown to no one ; the name of the sitter must never be mentioned ; and it must be completed as quickly as possible. To all these conditions Felix consented with a glad heart. The earl's manner softened by degrees ; he was evidently very fond of his daughter ; and he could not help feeling that the young artist was a gentleman, though less deferential in his manner than he should be to the head of the caste of Vere de Vere.

Nothing could be more cordial than the final chat between the two men ; each was pleased with the other ; and then, to Vereker's horror, everything was spoiled by a vulgar rap on the door, followed by the noisy entrance of Augustus Tothill.

The author was ill-dressed, ill-mannered, and altogether wanting in tact. Instead of standing aside quietly while Vereker and the earl said their parting courtesies, he first stared at the visitor, then twisted round on his heels, with something not far removed from a whistle, and, with his back to Lord Lillebonne, began to finger Vereker's curios.

Felix grew scarlet with rage; Lillebonne slightly paler with indignation. The latter put on his hat and stalked away, the former pursuing him down the ninety-eight stairs. Nothing was said until they were at the door, when Lillebonne stammered out, fiercely,

' I trust that you will have *no* visitors when my daughter is sitting.'

' I pledge you my honour,' Felix cried,

almost theatrically, ' that no one shall enter my room.'

' Thank you,' said the earl.

The brougham had been waiting in the shade, for the sun had conquered the mist. It was now brought across the road, Lord Lillebonne stepped into it, and was driven away. Vereker tore upstairs, three steps at a time, and burst in upon Tothill.

' Now, look here, Tothill, this is intolerable! How dare you come into my room in that rude manner, and behave to my visitor like an utter cad as you are? I'll thank you to be polite to anyone whom you may meet in my rooms, and, in fact, I'll thank you not to visit my rooms at all when I have other friends with me. You don't know how to conduct yourself in the presence of any decent man or woman.'

'Indeed!' said Tothill, coolly, 'is that your opinion? Pray how did your friend Lilebon behave to me at the Advance?'

'It is pronounced *Lillybun*. And so you suppose that Lord Lillebonne is bound to treat you with deference, *you?*'

'Yes,' returned Tothill, 'he would treat me with deference if he knew what I am about to do to him.'

'What is that?'

'I am going into Worcestershire to ferret out his family skeleton. If it is not to be found at Mont Veraye I shall go to Scotland and visit Strathtartan Castle. I'm in funds just now; I've had three articles in the May Mags, and I can afford myself a holiday. And I shall make my holiday pay, and make old Lillebonne pay.'

He had learnt at last how to pronounce the name.

' You mean to blackmail him ?'

' Not a bit of it. I would not stoop to such a thing. I prefer to work up the skeleton into an article——'

' An articulated skeleton,' put in Vereker, amused in spite of himself.

' ——And then I shall get it into one of the most scurrilous of the weeklies ; I shall call the owner of the secret the *Earl of Rosecake*, and his places *Mont Rather*, and *Strathplaid Tower*. The public will have no doubt as to whom I mean.'

' And an action for libel will ensue.'

' That will concern the publishers, not

me. Afterwards I shall look into the private histories of other noblemen. I shall write a second article; a third; perhaps a whole series; they will be collected into a volume, and I shall be known as the author of a standard work.'

Felix laughed. Tothill entirely believed in his own powers, and thought that only the opportunity was needed to enable him to become a great writer.

' You bloated democrat!' said Felix.

' I am certainly not an aris——'

' Aris—Tothill——' said Vercker.

' Neither aristocrat nor philosopher!' cried Tothill, ' but a man of the people, and a man of letters.'

' Then why do you wish to persecute Lord Lillebonne ?'

' I have no wish to persecute him; I

only want to make literary capital out of him. And this is really what brings me here to-day. If I get my papers on " Family Skeletons " brought out in one of the weeklies, I ought to have them illustrated. I thought that as you know this Lord Lillebonne you would make a drawing, or a caricature of him, which would illustrate the first paper of my series.'

' Thank you,' said Felix ; ' I don't caricature my friends.'

' Your friends ! Oh, come now, are you going to call old Lillebonne your " friend " ?'

' He is very friendly with me, and very kind. And I will not allow you to annoy him. Understand that.'

Felix was thinking that any annoyance

inflicted on Lord Lillebonne might also annoy his daughter.

Tothill, being without settled income, was naturally a democrat. He longed to take from others what they possessed: money, rank, position. If he had been the owner of even a thousand pounds in the Funds or any other stock, he would not have been anxious to do away with property.

'Why should old Lillebonne have all the roses and I all the thorns?' he cried. 'Why should he get up late and find the dew of the morning still awaiting him, while I must get up early if I want to snatch a cup of coffee at a breakfast-stall? Why has he all the good of life, and I all the evil?'

'Has he all the good and you all the

evil?' queried Vereker; 'has he half your talent?'

'No!' cried Tothill, going off on another tack; 'he has no talent. He is a bore in society, and a laughing-stock in the House of Lords. And I am a man who only wants the opportunity to make his mark. And that opportunity I am now going to make for myself out of his lordship's family skeleton. I am sorry you won't undertake the illustrations; it might be something in your pocket.'

'You are very kind,' returned Felix; 'but I, too, can make my own opportunity, and my own mark.'

'Yes, with your Lillebonnes as patrons,' said Tothill, with a sneer. 'Well, I've offered you a good thing, and you have declined. So good-bye.'

The author had got as far as the door when he turned back.

'I say, Vereker, do you know how much the fare is into Worcestershire?'

'Not exactly. You can calculate it at a penny-a-mile.'

'Ah! Now, I suppose your Lillebonne never travels anything but first-class. Well, say it is a hundred miles to Mont Veraye, hundred pence, eight and four-pence, say ten shillings. Then hotel-bill, fees to housekeeper at the place, etc., etc. Vereker, I'm rather hard up.'

'Why, you said just now that you were in funds.'

'So I am, for me. But this journey to Worcester, with another possible further journey to Perthshire, will take it out of me considerably. Would you mind lending me a sovereign ?'

'To help you to worry Lord Lillebonne ?'

'To help me to earn my living. Nothing pays now but personalities. Lend me the sov.'

Felix did so, feeling angry with Tothill, and sorry for him, and contemptuous of him. But he did not much believe that it would be in his power to annoy Lord Lillebonne; there was probably no skeleton at all; or, if a skeleton should be discovered and articulated, in all probability the editors and publishers would fight shy of Tothill's coarse personalities, and decline his article with, or without, thanks. At all events, if Tothill was out of town for a while, there would be no fear of his disturbing Lady Flora's sittings; and a sovereign was a low price to pay for his absence.

Augustus Tothill bursting into the studio while Lady Flora was sitting!——could a more appalling catastrophe happen to any artist? Felix shuddered as he pictured it. Certainly, Lady Flora, if not her father, should have the flowers without thorns, and the ' sweet wild scent,' and the dew awaiting her whether she rose early or late. All the best of the garden—of the world—should be hers. And even to think of the shabby, vulgar Tothill, the democrat, the penny-a-liner, as being in the same room with her, was afflicting to Felix Vereker, who was not in love with her, no, not one bit!

Then Coleman came in; and Felix began to wonder how he could keep Coleman out of the room when Lady Flora should be there.   The studio was as much Coleman's as Vereker's.   And yet Harry, though an excellent fellow in his way, was no fitting companion for the beautiful girl.   Vereker's anxiety on this point was soon removed.

'Congratulate me, old man !   The alderman has bought " Windsor." '

'I do congratulate you, warmly,' cried Felix.

'And more than that; he wants me to go down to Devonshire, where he has bought an old place near Lynmouth, and there paint half-a-dozen of the finest bits on his property.   Ain't that something like a commission ?'

'By Jove, it is !' said Vereker.

'I'm to go down at once, so as to get the spring foliage; and I'm to stay into the summer, so as to get the summer foliage. I should not wonder if I remain for the autumn tints. Hooray!'

Felix hoorayed too. Coleman's good fortune was also convenient for Vereker; Lady Flora would find the studio occupied solely by her painter. Nothing could fit in better.

'When do you go?' asked Felix.

'On Monday, I think; I want to have Sunday in London. I have an engagement for Sunday, if it be a fine day. And then on Monday I start off with bag and baggage for a glorious spell of work in the loveliest county of England.'

Felix said nothing of Tothill's journey and intentions; neither did he say anything about Lady Flora; Harry was too entirely happy in his own prospects to have any spare thoughts for others. He was not more selfish than most of us; at the same time he was not more unselfish. The same may be said of Felix Vereker.

CHAPTER IX.

ON THE RIVER.

Nature, animaux,
 Eaux, plantes, pierres,
Vos simples travaux
 Sont d'humble prières ;
  Vous obéissez ;
  Pour Dieu c'est assez.
                    VERLAINE.

A SUN-DAY indeed. A day with a brilliant, burning sun in the clear blue sky which seems so deep that one can gaze into it as into a blue lake, and yet never see an end to its depths. A day when, across this translucent sky, puffs of the flimsiest vapour flit; not clouds, but breaths of incense from spirits too fine for earth. And, like spirits, there are ' viewless voices ' singing incense-hymns in the air; careless of time and form, the larks fling out melody and harmony on the soft breeze. There is a tone of tender green on the margin of the stream, and a gauzy veil of green is flung over every tree. In quiet fields, and round the roots of reverend beeches, are primroses, pale and sweet; there are bluebells in the dells, and daisies on the lawns; there are buds on the rose-trees, and daffodils in the gardens; there is a freshness and a rapture in all Nature, and a gladness and a hopefulness in every human heart which is not black with ingratitude or with selfishness. Even the sick and sorrowful smile faintly, and the young and loving cannot speak what they feel; they obey their good impulses, that is enough.

Such a day brought all London out-of-doors. The rich people went down to Hurlingham, to Richmond, to Brighton; the poor people went to Kew, to Hampstead Heath, to Hyde Park. Henry Coleman went to keep his engagement with Edith Crane.

Apparently she had expected his visit. For she was dressed in her best frock and hat, and there was a little attempt at extra-adornment which did not escape his observant eye. Nellie, also, was looking very neat. Mrs. Crane had on an elaborate cap of lace and roses; and Joseph Crane leaned on the door-post, clothed in his best attire. As for Arthur, he was gone to the Sunday-school, and the baby was wrapped up in some red stuff. But Harry took little interest in Arthur and the baby.

'How do you do, Mr. Crane?' he cried, seizing the ex-postman's thin hand; 'do you remember my saying I would take you all on the river the first fine Sunday? Here is the fine Sunday, and there is the river.'

He pointed westward.

'I don't know as I am feeling well enough to go,' said Crane; 'you'd best go in and talk to my missus.'

The faces of Mrs. Crane and of the girls brightened as Coleman proposed his plan, which was to walk a little way and then take an omnibus, which would set them down close to the river, where they would find boats awaiting them. Edith coloured with pleasure; Nellie smiled. The mother's cap with roses was exchanged for a bonnet with feathers and tulips, the baby was swathed in a purple, knitted shawl, and the party descended to the hall-door.

'Are you going, then?' asked Crane, of his wife.

'Yes, we are all going, since Mr. Coleman is so kind. It will do you a world of good, Joe. I've brought down your scarf.'

'I don't know as I'm well enough,' he said, again; 'I find this warm weather very trying; I shall feel better when it's a bit cooler.'

'Oh, it's a lovely day, father!' cried Edith; 'I'm sure it will do you good.'

So he was persuaded, and they set off.

They caught an omnibus; the father, mother, and baby went inside; Harry and the two girls climbed up on the roof. They were set down close to Willow Green.

'That is my studio,' said Coleman, pointing up to his airy lodgings.

Then they arrived at the Green, where Howland was sauntering about, keeping an eye on the 'chaps and gals,' and on the 'prams' and the pipes, and all the various persons and things which crowded the green space within the white rails.

'Let me sit down a bit,' said Joseph Crane, as he edged himself on to a seat already fully occupied; 'how much further is it to the river?'

'About ten minutes' walk,' replied Coleman.

'Then I can't do it.'

Consternation fell upon his family.

'We will have a cab,' said Harry.

'No, it ain't no good. I could not stand the river or the motion of a boat. Let's put it off to next Sunday; I shall be stronger by that time.'

Edith and Nellie looked very sad.

'Oh, we will do both,' said Coleman; 'you can go home now, and come out next Sunday, and I'll take the ladies to-day.'

Mrs. Crane shook her head.

'I shall go home with him; he is not fit to go alone. Rest a bit here, Joe, and we will go home quietly by-and-by. He'll want my arm,' she added to Harry; ' he's as weak as a baby.'

'Shall we take baby?' Nellie asked of her mother, to Harry's infinite horror.

'In the boat without me?' exclaimed Mrs. Crane; 'no indeed, the blessed pet can't be taken without me!   And how I am to get your father home with him wanting my arm all the time, and how I am to carry the baby too, is more than I can say.   I wish we had never started.   Your father is not strong enough for jaunts like this.'

'No,' said Crane, feebly, 'I ain't strong enough.   If I'd had another month to get up my strength——'

Coleman was looking at Edith.   The girl's countenance was full of complex emotions; she was anxious for her father, sorry for her mother, disappointed for herself; she wanted to help her parents, and yet she longed to spend this beautiful afternoon in the pleasant way which had been promised her. Tears were not far from her eyes.

' Nellie must carry the baby,' said Mrs. Crane.

Nellie said not a word but took the little fellow in her arms. Her eyes were full of tears.

' At 'all events,' cried Harry, throwing one arm across Edith's shoulders in very owner-like fashion, ' you and I may go for our trip.'

The parents consented. It was a melancholy little procession, that of Joseph Crane leaning on his wife's arm and walking with languid, dragging steps, followed by Nellie, looking very sad, and overweighted by the sallow, sickly baby. It was an altogether forlorn party, turning away from the merry groups on the green,

and going back to dreary, indoor dulness.
Howland shook his head, and said to
Coleman,

'He's not long for this world, sir.'

Coleman feared that Edith had heard,
and hurried her on. She had heard; she
had known for some time that her father
was not likely to recover, but with the
light-heartedness of young people she
had not dwelt much on the fact. She
knew in a general, vague way that her
father would not live much longer. But
she was young, life was before her, she
had a lover, she had occasional pleasures,
the sky was often blue, the birds sang,
the flowers bloomed; death was a pale
shadow a long way off; at present this
shadow was not visible on her path. The
greatest gift of youth is its forgetfulness;

memory is the dearest gift of age, and only comes with age.

The banks of the river that day were but muddy flats edged with green here and there; the river was but an opaque liquid; yet never did Egyptian princess in her state-barge on the Nile, or peeress in her own right in her steam-launch under Cliveden Woods, enjoy herself more than did Edith Crane in an old wherry hired at 'a shilling the first hour and sixpence the second.' It was all horribly vulgar and stupid and common-place—ah, was it? Is beauty common-place, or talent, or man's devotion, and woman's love?

'I wish I was a rich man,' said Harry Coleman, resting on his sculls and letting the boat drift.

' Do you ?' said Edith ; ' you ought not to be discontented. What a lovely day it is !' she said, a little uneasy under his steady gaze.

' Yes, lovely.'

' Look at those boats, such a number, and girls in them all. And everybody looks pretty to-day.'

' In the matter of beauty, our boat is perfect,' said Harry.

Edith dipped her fingers in the water; Harry had not trusted her with the rudder-ropes.

' Oh, you flatter yourself !' she said, with a toss of her head, pretending to think that he included his own appearance in the beauty of the boat.

' What, I ?' he exclaimed; ' I am only your boatman.'

He looked still more fixedly at her; she tried to look at a lark singing high above human ken.

'Edith, if I were a rich man——'

'How pretty those bushes look!'

'——I would ask you——'

'Oh, what a lovely blue parasol!'

'——To be my wife directly, straight off. But being a poor man I can only ask you to wait until things improve. You are very young, Edith, you won't mind waiting, will you, dear?'

And then the girl turned upon him such a sweet face, with such a heavenly smile upon it, that Harry thought she was the loveliest creature on this summer earth. And she, seeing his earnest eyes and hearing his earnest voice, had not the slightest doubt but that he was the bravest, truest, grandest, noblest, wisest man that ever had existed or ever could exist. Yet she was but an ordinary pretty girl, and he was but an ordinary young man (not so very young either!) They were fulfilling the right impulses which the Creator had implanted in them as in flowers and birds, even in waters and stones, the impulses to be bright and happy, to gild labour with love, and to strengthen love with toil.

Edith was shy and coquettish, after the manners of her caste.

'Oh, how can you?' she giggled; 'now, don't talk like that.'

'I will talk like that,' Harry retorted, growing bolder; 'and I'll talk still more so!' Which threat he put in execution by telling her how long and how deeply he had loved her.

There was more than a score of young couples that day on the river, all saying much the same things; each of the girls was the fairest in the whole world, and each of the lads the noblest. There was even more than one elderly couple saying much the same things; but in their case the women were only charming and the men agreeable; for them superlatives were over.

' And the time can't be very far off,' said Harry Coleman, ' when the sweetest little girl in the world shall have her own little house, perhaps with a back garden, and her own drawing-room, and her own kitchen.'

' I should like a back garden,' said Edith, ' it is so convenient for drying and washing. And the parlour we could sit in when we had company. And if I had my own kitchen I could do such nice little bits of cooking.   Do you like orange fritters ?'

Harry adored them.

' And sardines on toast ?'

' The most delicious thing in the world for breakfast.'

And so they talked, as innocently as the larks in the high air.   Married life was to be a sort of game, a sort of make-believe of house-keeping, in which sovereigns and shillings would not be needed, in which the weather would be always May, and the time always afternoon.

And yet even this time was not always afternoon; five o'clock came, and Harry turned to go down-stream; and his slow strokes brought them by six o'clock to the landing-stage, where he disbursed two shillings for the most prosperous voyage which he had ever made in his life.

'Should you like tea now?' he asked of his companion.

'Oh yes!' What woman is not always ready for tea?

Coleman took his *fiancée* to the old-fashioned bay-windowed inn, where he and Vereker and Tothill so often took their ease; he placed her near the window from which she could see the sun sinking beyond the glittering river; before her was laid a tray, with not only tea but bread and butter, and eggs, and jam, and marmalade. And now, for the first time, Edith learnt whether her lover took sugar in his tea; a piece of knowledge most important and intimate, not to be revealed to the common mind. Never was feast more delicious. The sunset was rosy; so was life. So were Edith's cheeks. On either cheek burnt a sort of fire, delicate pink fire, which might have been a danger-signal to a man not in love with the daughter of the dying ex-postman.

Harry showed Edith the place where Felix had found Augustus Tothill contemplating the possibility, not of suicide, but of catching fish for his dinner; and he told her how that unappreciated author had taken a violent prejudice against the unoffending Earl of Lillebonne.

'Do you mean the nobleman where mother lived as young ladies' maid?'

'The same; and I understand that the

bloodthirsty democrat is going to hunt up some old story to the discredit of the de Veres, and to serve it up hot to some low weekly print.'

'How horrid!' said Edith; 'and how is he going to find out the story?'

'By investigations in Worcestershire and Perthshire.'

'Mother could tell him a good deal about the earl's family.'

'I daresay. But don't let her help him in his dirty work.'

'No,' said Edith, 'because mother was very fond of the young ladies. She says that Lady Flora Vere de Vere was the dearest child, and grew up a most amiable young lady.'

'She is a very pretty girl,' remarked Coleman, rather incautiously; 'nearly as pretty as somebody else whom I know.'

' Who can that be ?' said Edith.

They were now walking homewards. The pressure of Harry's hand answered Edith's question.

' Do you know that I am going out of town to-morrow?' Coleman asked; ' I have a commission from a very wealthy man, an alderman, to go down into Devonshire and paint pictures on his property. I shall be away a long time, my darling, but now that we have settled matters I don't mind going. And a couple of months will not seem long, after all; and I shall be making heaps of money, and when I come back I shall look out for that house with the back-garden. You don't mind my going, do you?'

'No-o,' said Edith; her lips quivered, and her heart sank.

Two months of nothing but her father's complaints and the baby's teething! Two months in the dreary garrets, two months of washing and cooking and posing as a model, while Harry was in the country with his easel and canvases, and enjoying himself from morning to night. Edith gulped down a sob. 'Men must work, and women must weep,' and it is all right. Women can no more be as happy as men than they can be as strong as men.

'Will you write to me?' said the poor girl.

'Of course, every day. And now, good-bye, my pet. When we meet again, I hope to have a bag of sovereigns in my pocket, big enough to buy the ring and all else that we shall want.'

' God bless you, Harry !'

They kissed. Edith stumbled up the dark stairs, her joy clouded by the sorrow of this early parting; Harry lit his pipe, and strolled home to the studios, feeling very brave and very happy.

CHAPTER X.

MONT VERAYE.

Nor sea, nor shade, nor shield, nor rock, nor cave,
Nor silent deserts, nor the sullen grave,
What flame-eyed Fury means to smite, can save.

FRANCIS QUARLES.

HAD Augustus Tothill been an explorer just landed on the shore of an unvisited continent, he could not have felt more virtuously energetic than he did on the morning after his arrival in Worcester. A congenial task was before him: that of working out everything to the discredit of an aristocrat. And beyond that task he had another in view: that of making himself famous by a book of scandalous memoirs. He had quite persuaded himself that to disclose the misdeeds of Lord Lillebonne and his ancestors would be a most praiseworthy enterprise, only less praiseworthy than that of making Augustus Tothill famous.

He came out from his hotel into the sunlit street of the provincial town. The head-waiter lounged at the door with a napkin flung over his shoulder.

'You say that the things to see are the cathedral, the china manufactory, and Mont Veraye. I shall easily find the cathedral and the china; where is Mont Veraye?'

The waiter advised Tothill to take the

train to the first station outside Worcester, and then to enquire further. This the author said he would do. He was in high spirits this lovely morning. He had money—an unusually large amount of it—for not only had two or three magazines paid him for the padding which he had supplied to them, but Vercker and some other acquaintances had lent him money. The previous evening he had dined well; this morning he had breakfasted well. In his hand was a reporter's note-book, in his mouth was a cigar; he started for Mont Veraye.

After ten minutes in the train, Tothill found himself at a very small station, where one young man was performing the duties of station-master, porter, ticket-collector, and pointsman.

'You go out by that gate,' said he, 'and up that road, and over the stile on the right, and along the footpath, and through the wood, and across the farm, and down the lane till you come to Mr. Smith's house. Then you go past the village till you come to Dr. Simpson's, and then you'll see the entrance to Mont Veraye.'

Guided by these instructions, Tothill went steadily on; the way was longer than he had expected; and by the time he reached the village, one o'clock had struck from the tower of the little church. It was time to get luncheon, which he proceeded to do at the village inn. Thus refreshed, he pursued his way to Mont Veraye.

A great iron gate flanked by two small ones gave access to Lord Lillebonne's park.

The gate-posts were of old, weather-beaten stone, and each bore the effigy of a lion, which was the cognizance of the house of Vere de Vere. Each lion clasped to his bosom a shield bearing the arms of the family: argent, on a fesse gules, three bezants of the first. Tothill made a grimace at these noble animals, and gazed up the long avenue. On either side of a broad road were beech-trees with silvery trunks and sweeping boughs. Beyond them on either side were stretches of exquisitely green turf dotted over with hawthorn bushes and horse-chestnut trees, now all in bloom. Here and there clumps of rhododendrons were purple with swelling buds. Lilac shadows lay among the thick foliage; herds of deer fed peacefully together; pheasants rose now and then

with a whirr and a shriek; doves cooed
unseen.

Tothill made some notes in his book,
and a rough sketch of the avenue. Next
he turned to the lodge. It was a low
cottage, built of grey stone, and had
creepers growing over it. Some poultry
scratched about at the side of it, and a
little mongrel white terrier ran out from
the open door, barked at the stranger, and
ran in again. A young girl came to the
door and looked at Tothill, and then re-
treated. Finally an old woman walked
out to the gate and stood staring at him
with the suspicious gaze of those who lead
lonely lives. Tothill thought he had better speak.

'Good morning,' he said, in his most
refined manner; 'pray, will you be good

enough to tell me if this is Mont Veraye ?'

' Yes, it be,' said the old woman.

' A beautiful property. A famous property. Happy is the man who possesses such an ancestral home !'

This ebullition brought no response. Only the girl came out and joined her grandmother in staring.

Tothill tried again.

' For such as me, poor dusty Londoner, it would be enough just to wander beneath these magnificent oaks.'

He was quite ignorant of everything pertaining to the country.

The girl smiled. The old woman said, ' Eh ?'

' Do you think his lordship would have any objection to my taking a stroll in the park ?'

' My patience me !' exclaimed the woman, with her thick midland accent, ' if that's what ye want, there's nought to prevent ye. His lordship could not keep ye out if he would; there's a right of way.'

With those contemptuous words she went indoors, and the girl stood smiling stupidly, while Tothill passed through one of the small gates and began to walk up the avenue.

Everything was so beautiful that for a while he forgot his malignant purpose, and merely enjoyed the scene. But when he came in sight of a red-brick, Elizabethan house, much restored and added-to, his spirit revived within him. There was the abiding place of the skeleton ! all the explorer, all the democrat, all the historian surged up in his bosom, and he was ready to pick the lock of the de Vere cupboard, and to drag out its nameless horrors into he light of day.

Tothill's ardour cooled a little when he saw a couple of gardeners at work in the flower-garden which lay glowing like a heap of gems in the afternoon sunshine. They paused and looked at him. One of them was the old woman's son, the other was the girl's brother. Tothill put on his best manners and approached them.

' Good-day, my men,' he said, supposing that to be the best-bred manner of addressing servants; ' fine weather for gardens.'

There was no reply.

' And fine gardens these. And a fine house. I have met his lordship in London.'

'Be you a new *vallet?*' asked the older man.

Tothill smiled affably.

'I have met his lordship at entertainments, galleries, and so forth. I have also met the countess and her daughters. Fine girls, both of them.'

'Be you the bootmaker from Malvern?' asked the younger man.

This was beyond a smile.

'I have met them in society,' said Tothill, with a very large S to the word; 'and I have a commission to visit this house and inspect its contents.'

The gardener shook his head.

'It is not a show-place, mister.'

'No, but by giving my card, I can see it.'

Tothill's commission was from himself;

his card was a written one, with his name and no address.

'Well,' said the gardener, 'ye can go and talk to the housekeeper, if ye like. Come on, Thomas, what about that lobelia?'

To attack the housekeeper was Tothill's next business. He walked up to the front door, a great massive, oaken portal, and rang a tremendous peal on the bell. This, he fancied, would prove impressive. It did, in fact, flurry the old woman who acted as housekeeper, or caretaker, at Mont Veraye in the absence of her master's family. She came panting to the door, and, knowing that the gardeners were on the lawn close by, she did not fear to draw back the bolts and face the enquirer. And now all Tothill's diplomacy was brought forward.

'Good *morning*,' he said, with a purpose,

for it is always *morning* until you go to dinner, and fashionable people like the Earl of Lillebonne, and Mr. Tothill, never dine until eight o'clock ; ' good *morning*. I suppose his lordship is not at home ?'

' No,' said the housekeeper, who at the first glance saw that Tothill was not what she called a gentleman.

' I thought not,' said the visitor, ' because I met him at a party the other day in London, and he did not say that he should be here at the same time with me. If he were here, he would show me all over the house.'

' We do not show the house,' remarked the old lady.

' Not to strangers, as I am well aware ; but of course his lordship would show it to a friend. It is an unlucky chance that he is not here. A delightful man is Lord Lillebonne, so refined and cultured; and Lady Lillebonne is a charming woman. As for the young ladies, they are quite the belles of the London season. Lady Clara is a regular beauty.'

' Yes, she is handsome enough.'

' Handsome enough to drive men out of their minds. Sad case that of young Laurence, very sad!' Tothill shook his head gravely.

But the housekeeper's face clouded over, and he saw that he was on dangerous ground. Gliding gently off it, he said,

' But, to tell you the truth, I admire Lady Flora more than her sister; a girl with a heart as lovely as her face.'

' She is a sweet young lady,' assented the housekeeper, her own withered yet rosy face growing bright with affection; 'Lady Flora is one that everybody must love.'

'I have met her at parties,' pursued Tothill, seeing that he had inserted the thin end of his wedge, 'and no more beautiful and charming girl have I met anywhere. I am not a dancing man, I am not even a marrying man, but for all that I can gaze upon Lady Flora until I long to dance with her. She will make a grand match one of these days.'

'Yes, sir, I make no doubt of it,' said the housekeeper, drawing back from the door and allowing Tothill to enter the large square hall; 'when they were here at Christmas, Mrs. Anderson said to me, "A good many young gentlemen cast their eyes on Lady Flora, I can tell you, Mrs. Pettit," says she; "but I can't make out that

her ladyship thinks of any of them," says
she. I should not wonder if Lady Flora
was to be an old maid; she never troubles
herself whether people are high or low,
rich or poor; so that she can help them
and do them good, and make them better
and happier, that is all she cares about.
And Mrs. Anderson sees it the same as I
do.'

'Well,' said Tothill, pleasantly, 'I am
neither high nor rich, but Lady Flora is
most agreeable to me. She is very anxious that I should see this house. You
see, Mrs. Pettit,' here he accidentally put
his hand into his pocket, and, also accidentally, clinked his money, 'you see I
am an author. I write books. I am going
to bring out a book which will have to do
with some old country-houses, and Lady

Flora would be much vexed if Mont Veraye were omitted. I ought to have brought a note from the earl, but I daresay my visiting-card will do well enough.'

He laid his card on a table in the hall, and Mrs. Pettit closed the door.

' I shall be very glad to accommodate any friend of Lady Flora's,' she said, ' and if you wish to see the house, sir, I will show you over it.'

Her earlier scruples were overcome by Tothill's plausible manner, by the chink of his money, and, above all, by the delight of having a stranger to talk to. She pointed out the figures in armour and the stags' horns, and the coats of arms displayed in the hall. Then she opened the door of a large, gloomy dining-room.

'These are family portraits,' she explained,

going through a list of names which had no interest for her listener, though they began with mythical Normans and down through ' the spacious times of great Elizabeth ' to Cavaliers and Georgian heroes, even to the small wigs and ruffles of the young nineteenth century, and the various costumes of the Victorian age. In the drawing-room, a bright apartment, were many beautiful bits of china, many ivory carvings, many miniatures. Tothill looked closely into the miniatures, and listened to Mrs. Pettit's long-winded stories about their originals. Battles and marriages, government employments and bishoprics, these seemed to be the chief materials of the de Vere family history. Not a hint of a bigamy, a forgery, a murder, a ghost, or a skeleton. Perhaps Mrs. Pettit purposely suppressed everything to the discredit of the family.

In going through the house, Tothill kept a watch for cupboards; he had a sort of notion that a material skeleton was hidden in a material cupboard. He saw several mysterious closets; and on enquiry found that one was Lady Betty's electuary closet, that another was the place where Colonel Henry de Vere had hidden from his Puritan pursuers; that a third had been the powdering closet of the Ladies de Vere in the reign of George the Third; but when he came round again to the hall, and had seen all the rooms which Mrs. Pettit was at liberty to show, he knew nothing to the discredit of the family.

He once more jingled his guineas, and made his last effort.

'Thank you very much indeed, my dear Mrs. Pettit, for all your kindness and information. I now shall be able to write an article speaking in glowing terms of this lovely park and house, with the towers of Worcester on one side, and the peaks of the Malvern Hills on the other. I need not allude to the sad story which attaches to the family.'

'I beg your pardon, sir,' said the old lady, drawing herself up.

'Every old and great family has its secrets,' remarked the author; 'the de Veres would not be a great family if they had not their troubles.'

'I do not understand you, sir,' said the housekeeper, stiffly.

'Of course, you are quite right not to gossip about it to everyone; but no doubt you are aware that the world is not so discreet as you are. *I* am discreet, my dear lady; you may trust to my discretion.'

He pressed her hand with such a confidential and sympathising clasp that she was mollified.

'No family, high or low, but has its trials, sir. I daresay the world knows a deal more about his lordship than his own people do. London has many tongues, and the country has few. But they all talk so loud in London that one can't hear what the other says. In the country they speak one at a time, and everywhere there is an echo.'

'Yes, yes; and it is a very sad story.'

'Very sad, sir; and a great trial to his lordship, and to her ladyship, which is a very haughty lady. But we hope that things are not so bad as they say, and perhaps the young man will see his folly, and do better as he gets older.'

Tothill had not an idea as to what she was alluding to, but he said, solemnly,

'Indeed, I hope so.'

'He must get tired of them after a time; I've never been inside a music-hall, or one of them low supper-rooms, and how a young gentleman, the eldest son of an earl, can take up with vulgar dancers and singers, quite passes me. If he was to marry a music-hall girl, it would pretty nigh kill his mother.'

'Let us hope for the best,' said Augustus Tothill, with a pious sigh; then, as his last shot, he put Lord Senlac and his naughty ways on one side, and added,

'Oh, by-the-by, I have not seen the mysterious, closed-up room.'

He saw a change on Mrs. Pettit's countenance.

'There is no closed-up room in the house.'

'Not? Why, that is one of the things which all London talks about. It is well known that Lord Lillebonne has a mysterious chamber, enclosing a great secret, and the eldest son——'

'Tut, tut!' cried Mrs. Pettit, growing vexed, 'there is nothing of the kind at Mont Veraye.'

Tothill caught the clue.

'Then London puts it in the wrong place. It is at Strathtartan Castle.'

'I have never been at his lordship's seat in Scotland.'

' But you are in the confidence of the family, my dear lady. (You do so remind me of my beloved aunt, Lady Tothill.) And you know of the mysterious room at Strathtartan.'

' I have only heard of it,' said Mrs. Pettit; she now had the door open for him to go out.

He saw that he should get no more information from her; so he again thanked her warmly, and put two half-crowns into her hand. She took them ungraciously, and closed the door as he departed.

' Well,' she murmured to herself, ' I was a stupid to take him for a gentleman. I never thought he'd give less than gold. And him wanting me to tell him about the closed door at Strathtartan Castle; why, I would not tell him if I knew. I am not in charge of Strathtartan; let him go to Strathtartan and talk to Mrs. Mac-Mullens, and see what he will get out of her. She is a Scotchwoman. Five shillings indeed!'

Tothill went slowly down the avenue; the air was hot and oppressive, and when he came to an inviting knot of old tree-roots which offered a quiet seat, he sat down and took stock of what information he had accumulated.

'None whatever,' he muttered, with his pipe between his lips, 'except that the skeleton is at Strathtartan, and I don't believe that old judy would have let that much out if I had not put her in a rage. And five shillings gone for that! dear at the price. Well, now, how can I make Mont Veraye pay? Can I use it for padding the first part of my article? A long and minute description of this fine old place, grounds and house; sketch of the head-gardener, portrait of the housekeeper. Armour, pictures, ivories, miniatures; winding up with "This is the Earl of Lillebonne's English country-seat, which does *not* contain the cupboard or the skeleton. Now, turn we to his Scottish property." That's your style.' As he had soliloquised, he had made rapid notes.

At that moment he heard a low growl of distant thunder. The sky was black in the south, and red overhead. Tothill was afraid of thunder. He jumped up and began to hurry towards the park gates, and then on to the station. Very quickly, within a quarter-of-an-hour, the storm was upon him. Dazzling flashes and rattling peals were around him.   Then down came the rain, drenching rain.   His thin garments were soon soaked through.   He reached the station in a dripping condition, and found that he must wait forty minutes for his train.   At the end of that time the sky had cleared, and his clothes had partly dried on him.

In the evening he found that he had taken cold, and next day he felt so ill that he remained in bed, doctoring himself with hot whisky and water.   This delayed his visit to Perthshire, and also did much towards emptying his purse.

CHAPTER XI.

THE FIRST SITTING.

You smile? why, there's my picture ready made,
There's what we painters call our harmony!
. . . .
Ah, but a man's reach should exceed his grasp,
Or what's a heaven for? . . .
How could it end in any other way?
You called me, and I came home to your heart.
Andrea del Sarto.   BROWNING.

IT never entered Lord Lillebonne's head that the young man whom he employed to paint his daughter's likeness could fall in love with her. He was superbly confident that this matter of the portrait was

as entirely without sentiment as the purchase of a mantle at Howell and James's,
or as a morning ride in the park. The
shop-assistant at Howell and James's could
not lift his eyes to Lady Flora Vere de
Vere, nor could the groom behind her in
the park dream of flirting with the young
lady; even so nothing beyond business
relations could arise over the sittings at
Willow Green Studios.

The earl chose to forget that there have
been ladies of good family who have
eloped with shop-assistants and with
grooms, who have married bakers and
trainers, and even painters. But he
chose to ignore those facts, and to believe
that his daughter was perfectly safe in
the society of the young artist. Had
Lady Lillebonne been told of the sittings

her womanly instinct would have been alarmed, and she would have done her duty as chaperon to Flora. But the matter was kept a secret from her. She was so much occupied in the pursuit of Sir Ronald Stanley, whom she intended to make her son-in-law, that she was quite satisfied on hearing that Flora went out two or three mornings a-week with her maid.

'When Clara is married,' she said to herself. 'I will look more after Flora. Meanwhile, she is quite safe with Anderson.'

For Anderson was a very discreet person.

Lord Lillebonne came with his daughter to the first sitting. He began to mount the ninety-eight steps, and she came after him. But before they had got twenty steps, they met Felix Vereker on the lookout for them. He expressed his sorrow at the height of the ascent, his gladness at their arrival, his hopes for success, and his fears of failure.

When he got them into his room, he placed chairs for them until they had recovered their breath; as for himself, ten steps or a hundred made no difference to his vigorous heart and lungs. He had arranged a screen, and behind it a dressing-table and glass, a comb and brush, and a powder-puff, all for the use of his sitter. No such arrangement had been made for Edith or Nellie Crane.

Next came the decision as to full-face, three-quarter-face, or profile. Flora's nose was ' tip-tilted,' and Felix did not wish a profile; her cheeks were rather too plump for actual beauty, and Lillebonne did not wish a full-face. So they settled on three-quarters.

The question of costume came next. Flora was wearing a warm but dark-green gown of mixed woollen and satin stuff. It was made open at the neck, and the sleeves ended at the elbow. She had brought with her a scarf of pink gauze which she twisted round her throat and left floating across one arm, in such a way that all the hard edges of the gown were obliterated. With this costume Vereker was quite contented; the green suited well her brilliant complexion, and the pale pink gauze seemed to blend the green of the dress, with the pink of her skin. When the girl was at length seated and settled, her cheeks flushed with natural vanity, and her lips smiled with innocent pleasure; Felix felt that he could work on this portrait with double the enthusiasm which had fired him for the 'Apple Blossoms' and the 'Buttercups.' Nellie's picture was nearly finished, and its completion was in a very near future.

Now began the first rough sketching with charcoal. The earl stood beside the easel and made remarks which were in no wise helpful to the artist. By degrees the conversation became easier, and the National Gallery was spoken of, and the Louvre, and the treasures in Venice, in Florence, and in Rome. Then books were discussed; and music. And Lord Lillebonne felt a sort of condescending surprise when he found that not only did Felix

Vereker drop no h's, but that he was actually well-read, and acquainted with many things outside his profession. If the young man had been English, and had been in some profession—the Bar, for instance—in which he was not likely to make any money, he would have been quite presentable in society.

The first sitting was a preliminary one. Flora was soon tired, and Felix was so excited that he had hardly full command of his eye and hand. Lillebonne was greatly bored after the first half-hour, and made up his mind that for the future he would not act chaperon, but send Anderson instead. He and Felix had talked about foreign travel and Irish politics, and ecclesiastical discipline and many other things. Flora had listened, surprised to find that the artist was as much acquainted with these matters as her revered father, who had put on his 'House of Lords' manner. And then conversation flagged, and Lord Lillebonne seemed impatient, and Flora weary.

'I think that will do for to-day,' said Felix, laying down his implements.

'Put on your bonnet, my dear,' said the earl briskly, to his daughter; 'I want to get home and look up the *Colonial Dog-tax Act* before I go down to the House.'

While Flora was putting on her bonnet, Lord Lillebonne glanced about the studio and enquired what work Mr. Vereker had in hand.

Felix pointed out the 'Buttercups,' and said, carelessly,

'I have only that in hand, and an en-

larged reproduction of a family-portrait.
Would you care to see it ?'

'I will not trouble you,' replied Lillebonne; his idea of Vereker's 'family-portrait' was of a stout woman in black
satin and a black cap studded with red
ribbons; her huge hand displayed fingering a thick gold chain; her cheeks ver-
milion, her hair in ' sausage curls.'

Vereker's relatives were probably of the
shop-keeping class, grocers, bootmakers,
haberdashers; highly respectable, but not
interesting, and none the more interesting
because they were American.

Again Vereker felt irritated by Lillebonne's manner; it was not discourteous,
it was not rude, but it was calmly indiffer-
ent, as if from the height of his position
he could really not perceive so small an

object as a young painter's ' family.'
Felix stiffened visibly; but as Lady Flora
re-appeared from behind the screen,
smiling and lovely under a shady hat, he
unbent once more, and hastened to open
the door and escort her down the stairs.

On the stairs they met Nellie Crane,
who did not know anything about Lady
Flora de Vere.

' Please, Mr. Vereker,' said the child,
' I have come——'

' I can't attend to you now,' replied
Vereker, hastily ; ' go up and wait for
me.'

Flora had seen that the young girl was
pretty.

' Is that one of your sitters ?' she
inquired.

' One of my models.'

Flora did not condescend to say anything more, but it struck her that Felix Vereker was but a young man, and that he had some very attractive models.

' My daughter will come next Friday at the same hour,' Lord Lillebonne was saying ; ' I do not know that my engagements will allow me to come with her, but in that case her maid will accompany her.'

Vereker bowed. He was vexed to see not only Quekett at the entrance, with his brooms and his cloths, but also Mrs. Quekett, half in hiding, peering round at the beautiful young lady.

' Where shall we find a cab ?' asked his lordship, in a helpless tone.

' I think there will be one on Willow Green. Allow me to look out for Lady Flora.'

Felix ran to the end of his street, and at one of the houses on Willow Green he saw a hansom which had just set down a fare. He whistled—rather vulgarly, as the earl thought—and so summoned the cab. He assisted Lady Flora to climb into it; he spoke the address to the driver, and stood with two fingers up to his forehead as if saluting. For, not having on a hat, he could not take it off.

When they had been driven away, Felix turned from the thought of his visitors to be vexed with the Queketts; brooms and dusters in the hall just as a beautiful lady was coming out! A stout woman in a dirty apron peeping round a corner when Lady Flora Vere de Vere was passing by!

'Now, look here, Quekett,' the young

man began, 'when my sitters are passing through the hall——'

'Yes, sir,' said the porter, 'if I'd a-knowed, I'd a had it cleaned up earlier. But you gents come in and out all day, and never think of the scraper.'

'Well, don't bring your brooms again into Lady—a lady's—way.'

'No, sir. I see she was very well dressed, that young lady. She ain't a model, I suppose, Mr. Vereker?'

'She is not,' answered Felix, almost fiercely.

'If she had told me her name, or the old gentleman's either, I might have announced her properly. They come in without ringing for me, and they gave me no card to take up, so what could I do?'

'You did quite right; all except the brooms.'

'Next time she comes, what shall I say, sir?'

'Her name's of no consequence,' said Vereker, in his sternest manner.

Mrs. Quekett came forward.

'Leave the young lady to me, Quekett, and get to your work. That gas-lamp up there is disgraceful, simply disgraceful. You get up them steps and clean it directly, or I'll call the attention of the directors to it, and you'll hear what they will say. And now, Mr. Vereker, I'm at your service, and the next time Miss— Miss Whatsername comes here, you let me know, and I'll be ready to wait on her.

'There is no need of your services,' said Felix, running up the stairs.

Mrs. Quckett harangued her husband on the subject of 'unknown young women coming to sit to young fellers like that Vereker; she did not know what the world was coming to; gals do things in these days that would have made their grandmothers die of horror.' Quckett agreed with every word that his wife said.

Felix had forgotten that Nellie Crane was in his studio. He found her standing before the canvas on which only an outline of a head and bust was visible.

'Oh!' said the child, 'you can never mean that for the beautiful lady whom I met on the stairs!'

'There is not much likeness at present,' said Felix; 'what do you want, Nellie?'

'Please, Mr. Vereker, I came to ask if you would like me to sit to you again.

We are very badly off just now, and I do so want to earn some money. Father was taken with a fainting-fit yesterday, and when the doctor came he said we were to get brandy and port wine and beef-tea and everything to keep up his strength.'

'I am very sorry,' said Felix; ' but you know " Buttercups " is nearly finished, and I don't think I can paint you again.'

'Nor Edith? She has got an engagement to sit to a lady at Notting Hill, and if I could get one we should not do so badly. And we don't think Baby can live.' This she said in quite a hopeful tone.

'I am very sorry,' Felix said again. He did not know what else to say.

'And Edith is keeping company with Mr. Coleman, and he has gone into the country, and has only written once to her,

and she thinks that he is forgetting her
already.'

'Oh, he won't forget her, never fear.
Look here Nellie, I'll give you a note to a
man whom I know, and ask him to employ
you as a model.   He keeps a sort of School
of Art, and may give you an engagement.
I don't know what else to do for you.
When is your sister to be married to Mr.
Coleman ?'

Nellie shook her head.

'Oh, not for a long time. Mother could not
spare her at present. She does half mother's
sewing. If father was taken, there would
not be nearly so much to do or to spend,
and very likely Edith could get married
then.   The doctor says he can't last much
longer.'

' Poor fellow !' said Felix.

He gave Nellie the introduction to Mr. Oscar Burne Grafton, who did find an engagement for her; and thus absolute starvation was staved off from the Crane family. When he was alone, Felix sat down and thought about the ex-postman and the hereditary disease which was killing him, and how probable it was that his children would develop the same complaint in some form. And he felt very sage as he shook his head over Coleman's folly in tying himself to such a hopeless family. Then he reflected that hardly any family is entirely free from some taint of body or mind; even the de Veres were said to have a family secret; the sweet, charming Lady Flora might be the heritress of some terrible malady or disgrace. And that wretched, ill-conditioned Tothill had set himself to the task of discovering that malady or disgrace. Might his intentions be frustrated, Felix earnestly prayed.

And then the artist turned to his canvases; began some background colouring for Flora's fair head; put in some shadows to his ' family portrait ' of the lady in blue and gold-spotted gauze; and afterwards went out to try if he could find a dealer who would buy ' Buttercups,' or at least allow it to stand in his gallery on sale, as soon as it should be finished.

END OF THE FIRST VOLUME.

Printed by Duncan Macdonald, Blenheim House, London, W.